A Brace of Skeet

A Brace of Skeet

Gerald Hammond

St. Martin's Press
New York

c.1

M

Library of Congress Cataloging-in-Publication Data

Hammond, Gerald.
    A brace of skeet / by Gerald Hammond.
        p.   cm.
    ISBN 0-312-04688-X
    I. Title.
PR6058.A55456B73   1990
823'.914—dc20   90-37275
                                                                CIP

First published in Great Britain by Macmillan London Limited

First U.S. Edition: October 1990

10   9   8   7   6   5   4   3   2   1

As far as I know, there is neither a Moorfoot Loch Reservoir nor a Pentland Gun Club. The latter and all its members are intended to be entirely fictitious.

While this story was in preparation, fresh legislation affecting shotguns was being bludgeoned through Parliament. Since the only thing certain about the final outcome was that the new regulations would have no downward effect on the use of firearms in crime, I have preferred to assume that the story dates from before the new legislation.

ONE

The task of telling this story seems to have landed in my lap. Dad, who, at the drop of a hat, will burst into print on such subjects as ecology, ballistics or the history of the firearm, never descends to what he thinks of as mere anecdotage and he was abroad when all this happened. Simon, who usually writes up Dad's more spectacular cases, is dashing madly about, researching for a biography of the Reverend Alexander Forsyth. And, as the clincher, it happened to me. Or perhaps I made it happen to myself – and might have died for my stupidity. So I seem to be elected.

When I was a child, I thought that my Dad was the bravest man on earth. I still do in a way, although I also agree with Mum that his courage is made up with more than a smidgeon of rashness. Several times I have seen him face up to an armed man and once even to Mum when she had lost her temper with him. His pride never lets him back away. Perhaps that's what rashness is.

Which makes it all the odder that this paragon of courage is terrified to fly. From the safety of the ground he can watch planes zooming past or scratching white lines across the sky without ever doubting their ability to stay up there; but on the rare occasions when he has been induced to go up in one he has known for a fact that nothing so cumbersome and illogical could possibly support his weight. This delusion is especially strange in a man who has made a lifelong study of ballistics and so should have some feeling for the effects of airflow, but when we did Physics in school and I tried to explain the Venturi Effect to him he only said that, if any competent engineer could prove that a bumblebee couldn't possibly fly, no doubt he could prove the converse about aircraft.

The result of Dad's phobia was that for years the few foreign holidays that he and Mum managed to take usually consisted of a long drive, a Channel crossing and another and longer drive down through France. And even then, Dad being Dad, the holiday usually turned into a business trip around the gun centres. Which was all very well for Dad but a bit hard on Mum, who would rather have lolled on a beach or hit the nightspots. Mum can be a swinger when she gets the chance.

It all came to a head earlier this year. Mum was more than a little run down after a dose of 'flu, and the doctor, a serious young man who had just joined the practice almost straight from college, told her that she was overdue for a proper holiday.

For years, Dad had been hankering to cross the Atlantic. He wanted to see Mexico, and some American friends had offered to fly down and take him on a dove hunt – which in Mexico, I gather, is really something.

Everybody decided that now was the hour for him to do it instead of talking about it and they ganged up on poor Dad. By everybody, I mean Mum, Dad's partner Wallace and Wallace's wife Janet. I stayed on the side-lines. I understand about phobias – I don't mind flying, but no way could I take a spider out of the bath. And Ronnie, my only uncle, who doesn't understand about holidays anyway, was not consulted. But the others were adamant. He was overdue for a holiday and he was going to have one and enjoy it whether he wanted to or not.

Dad gave in with a good grace and even volunteered to go and make the necessary arrangements with the travel agent. When he returned, his unusual compliance was explained. He had arranged the Atlantic crossings by way of a cruise ship, thus extending their absence by almost another month, and had charged the considerable expense

8

against the firm. Wal was too relieved to complain; Dad is an excellent gunsmith and brings a lot of money into the firm by dealing in quality guns, mainly antiques, but he will insist on meddling in what Wal regards as his own province – the management of the shop and accounts. Mum, who was getting a lot more holiday than she had bargained for, was delighted.

I could easily have gone to stay with Janet and Wal, who have the flat above the shop in Newton Lauder; but Dad's workshop and the stock of antique guns are in our home at Briesland House, about two miles outside the town. It was decided that, even after the best of the guns had been lodged at the bank, the house would still make too good a target for a burglar. I was to stay in the house. But Briesland House is rather isolated, a couple of miles from the small town of Newton Lauder in the Scottish Borders. So it was further decided that my uncle would move in with me to see to my safety. (When he objected that his cottage would then be vulnerable to any passing burglar, Dad retorted that any self-respecting burglar would have to be paid to take any of Ronnie's treasures away.) Janet was appointed to supervise the physical and moral wellbeing of the pair of us.

Dad worked like a demon for a fortnight and, by the time of their departure, his side of the business was right up to date. From there on I was expected, in addition to helping Wal and Janet in the shop, to do my best to keep it that way; but Dad was insistent that anything difficult be farmed out to a friend of his in Edinburgh. Dad still forgets that, although I served my time as an engraver, I can polish a stock, make and temper a spring, do colour hardening, fit a new part or, if all else should fail, make and case-harden it myself. After following him around – 'like a puppy-dog', Mum always says – ever since I was old enough to toddle, insisting on joining in whatever he was doing and eternally asking questions, I could hardly have helped learning the tricks of the trade.

After spending money on a good education for me, my parents had been hesitant about letting me join the family business, but I can be as stubborn as Dad and they soon saw that I would never be useful at anything else.

If a preoccupation with guns seems to the more chauvinistic reader to be unnatural in a young woman, I can only say that, quite apart from Dad's influence, my interest was first attracted by the sheer beauty of polished wood and engraved metal and the clean, functional lines. And that, I seem to remember, was before we had even discovered that I had the straight eye and natural co-ordination which go to make a good shot. Women may not have the same urge to gather meat as do men – although I can and do shoot game or wildfowl with some of the best of them – but they can certainly become competent shots. When I won my first medal at the clay pigeons, I was hooked.

The cruise ship could hardly have passed Fastnet Rock before it was made clear that my help in the shop would only be required for emergency cover. Janet and Wal could manage very well between them, thank you very much.

I don't know from whom I inherited my innate honesty, the cause of the trouble. (Certainly not from Dad, who falls well within the definition of a lovable rogue.) It offends my nobler instincts to sell a refined and delicate product to a customer when his needs would be better met by something cheaper and more robust. Such a deal seems to be an insult to the product as much as to the customer. Wallace came back to the shop unexpectedly, to overhear me gently but firmly steering a lady who wanted a birthday present for a wildfowling son, away from a very expensive and high-powered pair of binoculars – which he could never have held steady without a tripod – and towards a light but solid, rubber-covered pair of ten-powers at a fifteenth of the price.

With only a trickle of guns coming in for attention, I found myself more or less a lady of leisure; and this suited me admirably. I loved my parents, but the restraints imposed through their delayed realisation that I had at last grown up often rankled. There were many more interesting things to do than stand behind a shop counter or climb the ladder to the highest shelves in search of goods which the local lads had no intention of buying but had only asked about in the hope of seeing up my skirt.

Ronnie, my uncle, is usually fully committed to his job as Sir Peter Hay's stalker-cum-ghillie. But the continuing fine summer had spoiled the fishing and Ronnie had already made his quota of culls. Sir Peter had other work for him. When the young policeman tracked us down, he found us killing rats around a chicken farm, aided by three terriers, twelve ferrets and a black Labrador – the last in a purely advisory capacity, because ratting can harden a gundog's mouth.

We were having a lovely time, accounting for a whole lot of rats while at the same time winning and losing small bets on the performance of individual dogs as the hundreds of different holes were cleared. I was almost 25p ahead when the shadow caught my eye and I looked round. A uniformed constable was watching patiently from the corner of the nearest shed.

I ignored him until the immediate rush was over and the ferrets were surfacing again before pointing him out to Ronnie. 'I think they've come for you,' I said. 'Not before time. Have you been on the rampage again?'

'No' for weeks,' Ronnie said seriously. 'I'm overdue.'

The constable approached us, stepping carefully through the dust and litter. 'Miss Deborah Calder?' he asked, as though he had difficulty believing it. 'The Chief Super wants to see you. Urgent, he said it was.' He was not exactly good looking, but he was well built and his face was round and friendly. 'You missed one,' he added. 'It ran under yon wee shed.'

'I saw it. *Mousus tomandjerricus*. You don't often get them among brown rats,' I told him.

11

'I jalouse they've found out about you-know-what,' Ronnie said in tones of doom. He spoiled the effect with a broad grin.

'I doubt it. Mr Munro probably just wants a quick fumble in the back seat, same as usual,' I said. 'I'd better go. He gets fractious when he's kept waiting for his fun.'

The constable looked slightly shocked at this *lèse majesté*, but Ronnie only laughed. My uncle is a rough diamond who looks much as one of the Easter Island statues would look if squashed down a bit. The general view of the family is that he should be kept in a dark cupboard and only let out to frighten children, but I like him. I can say things to him which would bring down the wrath of God if I said them at home.

I gave Ronnie my stick, gathered up one of his ferrets for him before it could go back underground, whistled up Sam the Labrador and then went to look for the constable, who seemed to have vanished. I found him using the radio in a panda car parked in the yard behind the farmhouse.

'The Chief Super says we're to meet him at Marthasfield,' he said.

I put Sam on the back seat of the panda and sat in the front. Sam is really Dad's dog, but Sam thinks that he is mine and I am inclined to agree with him. 'I want to go home and change,' I said.

'Can't keep the big chief waiting.'

'Yes, I can. Easily.'

'Uh-uh,' the constable said.

'Well, at least I can wash,' I said. 'Rats carry all sorts of diseases. Wiele's disease, for one – the dreaded Ratter's Yellows. Stop at the first pub or I'll bite you and pass it on.'

He was turning out to be a bit of a prune. He was a polite young man but very shy and terrified of putting a foot wrong. He denied knowing what Chief Superintendent Munro wanted with me, although I'm sure that he could have made a good guess. He let me off at a pub

12

but refused to park within a hundred yards of it. At least I was able to clean up a bit before we met Mr Munro at Marthasfield and the constable had lent me a comb.

Mr Munro was waiting at the roadside in the back of a police Jaguar. The car was complete with uniformed driver, so I knew that this was very official business. I said a polite goodbye to my constable and got in beside Mr Munro, who was in full uniform with silver bits all over it. The car moved off before I was properly settled. Sam, who had dived in at the last moment, sprawled across our feet.

'What's the hurry?' I asked. 'Has there been a murder?'

He smiled his twisted smile. I have known Mr Munro since he was a chief inspector, and Dad has known and squabbled with him for even longer. Sometimes you would think that they hated each other, and then, when it suited them and usually when you least expected it, they would form a sudden alliance against the rest of the world. Personally, I'd always got on well with him. I respected him and yet he always made me feel at ease. He was a tall and gangling Hebridean from the outermost corner of Benbecula or Harris, very stiff and prudish but with a tiny streak of humour like one of those streams running deep underground but finding a way to the surface when conditions were just so. I had always thought of him as nearing retirement, but here he was, still around and now the big cheese for our part of the Scottish Borders.

'A murder?' he said. 'Perhaps that is for you to tell us. Some of my colleagues wish to speak with you.'

I reviewed the last few months and could not remember killing anybody, or even witnessing anything which could possibly relate to any crime. 'Before I meet anybody,' I said, 'I must go home and change.' I was dressed for ratting, in jeans, a T-shirt with a mildly rude logo on it and my hair pulled back with a rubber band.

'You are better as you are,' he said. 'You may not be dressed up for a social occasion but at least you look for

13

once like a serious and practical person.' The quaint lilt in his voice emphasised, as always, the precision of his words. Dad swears that Mr Munro still thinks in the Gaelic and translates into English as he goes along, but Dad says that Mr Munro still has peat between his toes. I think that he has never lost the speech patterns learned from elders who spoke that way.

'So what's it all about?' I asked.

He answered a question with a question, as is the habit of policemen. 'What can you tell me about the Pentland Gun Club?'

As it happened, I could have told him a great deal. In my youth I had earned pin-money trapping, scoring and generally making myself useful while Dad was shooting there. Later, I had often practised and competed on their layouts. I had also read every book in Dad's considerable library – even, during a convalescence, the ones whose footnotes had footnotes of their own. If I had to answer some of his questions in order to get answers to my own, so be it.

'It's a big club,' I explained, 'very old and very prosperous. It started out as a live pigeon trap-shooting club in Edinburgh, in the days when that was legal and there used to be huge betting on it. In the mid-nineteenth century it was one of the first clubs to use the newfangled glass balls filled with feathers as targets. In 1880 a man named Ligowski produced the first clay pigeons, but they were very hard to break because they really were—'

'Very interesting,' Mr Munro said patiently, 'but could we not perhaps come a little more up to date?'

I seem to have inherited Dad's habit of lecturing instead of telling the listener the little that he really wants to know. People never do seem to want to know much about anything interesting. 'Right,' I said. 'The club owned a whole stretch of land and Edinburgh grew up around it. About twenty years ago, they were compulsorily purchased out of it for a sum which was huge even then.

There's a hotel and a shopping centre standing on it now.

'So the club took the money and ran. They bought their present site, on the bank of Moorfoot Loch Reservoir. Dad says that the Scottish Office leaned on the local authorities to give them outright planning permission, just to get them out into the wilds where the noise wouldn't be bothering anybody. They built themselves a classy set-up – clubhouse, Skeet layout with stone trap-houses and safety walls, Sporting stands with a high tower, Down the Line, and electrically operated Laporte traps everywhere you look.'

Mr Munro was visibly struggling to keep up. 'These traps,' he said. 'They are for throwing clay pigeons?'

'That's right. The nomenclature,' I explained, 'still comes from the old days of live pigeon shooting. They were released from one of three traps operated by a boy who pulled a string, so the call for a bird – they're still called "birds" – is "Pull". Actually, you're supposed to call "Mark" or "Ready" in some disciplines, but "Pull" is accepted almost anywhere. The dead bird had to fall within the marked circle or it didn't count.' I saw from his face that I was lecturing again so I shut up.

'It sounds expensive,' Mr Munro commented. 'Does it cost much to be a member?'

'The subscription isn't much,' I said, 'but the entrance fee's heavy. It has to be. You can't let any old tink walk in off the street, pay a year's subscription and own part of all the assets. But clay shooting always costs. Cartridges aren't cheap, good equipment costs the earth and entry into competitions has to cover prize-money except in the big-time when it's sponsored.'

Mr Munro was looking a bit dazed. 'These are rich men, then?'

'Not necessarily. Dad's been a member since the year dot. Of course, he joined before the club moved and the entrance fees went up. I don't know if you'd call him rich.'

15

It occurred to me that the Chief Superintendent, coming from his background among the peat bogs and cottage weaving, probably would call him rich although Dad would have gone to the stake denying it. 'Non-members can still use the facilities or get some coaching on a day-ticket,' I added. 'It's frowned on by the CPSA but winked at by everybody else. Now, what's it all about?'

He pretended not to hear my question. 'Do they hold some of the big competitions? Championships and the like?'

'Almost never. They host some charity shoots occasionally. But mostly the facilities are used for practice, coaching and friendly, informal competitions at weekends. Game shooters sharpening up for the season and top-level competitors getting ready for the big competitions elsewhere. Very relaxed and casual and great fun. Now, either tell me what this is about or take me home.'

He looked at me reproachfully. Policemen hate to tell you what something is all about. 'There has been a dead man found there. I know no more than that, so there is no use you asking me any more questions. It is outside my territory. There was some disagreement as to whether it could have been caused by an accident, so they telephoned me and asked me to bring along my tame expert.'

'But that's Dad,' I said.

'I know that well. But in his absence, you can deputise for him. You have shown in the past that you have the knack of it.'

Mr Munro had always pretended to believe, or else laboured under the delusion, that Dad's successes owed more than a little to my help. Dad's curiosity and his insatiable interest in anything to do with guns or their ballistics had involved him in a number of investigations of crimes involving firearms, sometimes on the side of the law but, because forensic laboratories are often under the control of the police, more usually on behalf of the defence. Once or twice, good luck had helped me to lay my childish finger on the crucial question to ask, which only goes to show that if you fire enough shots you'll hit something in the end. Before I could protest that I was hardly qualified to advise the police, the Chief Superintendent was speaking again.

'I am surprised that it has not happened before,' he said, severely. 'A whole *bourach* of grown men with shotguns all blazing away at moving targets.'

I had forgotten how anti-shotgun Mr Munro had always been. It was the one subject on which he and Dad could be counted on to get into furious argument.

'It isn't like that at all,' I said, trying not to laugh. 'It's all very disciplined, with people shooting one at a time and strict rules about emptying the gun before turning round. Anybody waving a gun about gets sent home straight away. Even on the Christmas Eve shoot . . .' I stopped. There was nothing to be gained by fuelling Mr Munro's belief that all shotgun owners were mad if not actually criminal.

'Tell me about the Christmas Eve shoot,' he said quickly.

On second thoughts, it was always easy and rather fun to shock the Chief Superintendent. 'I've never been to it,' I said. 'It's the one occasion of the year when it's strictly Men Only. But Dad's told me about it. There's a running buffet; but there's also a teetotal safety officer appointed, and he has absolute power to stop anybody shooting who's had enough to affect his safe performance.

'There's usually a good turnout. They have several small handicap competitions for prizes of Christmas goodies. Then, for the main event, they each put a ten-penny piece in the kitty for every pair of shots. They shoot easy doubles off the tower and whoever misses a bird drops out.'

'And the last man left in collects the kitty?'

It was a shame to have to correct him just when he was sure that he was catching on. 'Unless the kitty's been won before then,' I said. 'You see . . . did you know that a

17

clay pigeon is sort of hollow underneath? It's shaped like a small straw boater.'

'I will take your word for it,' he said.

'Thank you. Well, on Christmas Eve, among the stacks of clays loaded into the magazine of the automatic trap, quite a large number have had items of ladies' underwear inserted, held in with a piece of cardboard. When the clay's broken, that's left floating in the air and a cheer goes up.'

'A terribly expensive and wasteful proceeding,' Munro said, sternly. The waste seemed to offend him more than the sexist humour.

'That nylon stuff's only pennies at sale time,' I said, 'and most of it can be used over and over again. Who's going to notice pellet holes in cheap lacework? Anybody getting a bra and a pair of panties in the air at the same time scoops the kitty. Then they finish up with a drinking session and several minibuses take them home.'

The Chief Superintendent sat dreaming. As a true Highlander, the drinking would not have offended him as much as the frivolous expense. His Calvinist conscience may have been unable to compete with the mental picture of a sky filled with floating lingerie.

But after a minute of contemplation he shook off his enchantment and, as the car climbed the slopes of the Moorfoot Hills from farmland to moors, he questioned me closely about the different disciplines of clay pigeon shooting.

The Moorfoot Hills are dotted with reservoirs, but while Portmore Loch, Gladhouse Reservoir and the others are to the north and serve Edinburgh and its satellites, Moorfoot Loch Reservoir itself was formed in a valley in the southern slopes to provide water for Peebles and Galashiels and as far as Newton Lauder.

Our road was narrow but in good order. It brought us up to the left of the dam and suddenly a whole new tract of scenery opened up. The sails of several dinghies dotted the water. A sprawling complex of buildings showed up at the far end of the reservoir, perhaps a mile away. The buildings were modern in design, jolly to the point of being skittish in character, and yet managed to make concessions to the countryside by lavish use of stone and timber.

'That place is new since I last came this way,' Mr Munro said. 'What is it?'

'Leisure complex,' I said. 'Timeshare units and a country club. They have horses and squash and tennis, and those dinghies. You can't see it from here, but there's a golf course beyond. The first stage was only finished about a year ago and already they're planning the next extension. Some of the occupiers turn up to shoot at the Gun Club. One or two of them are members.'

The Chief Superintendent grunted. 'Whatever next?' he said. 'Tell me about Skeet.'

Our road swung away from the reservoir and then ran parallel to the waterside. We entered a gateway in a wire fence, not far short of the Leisure Complex. A gravel drive brought us to the clubhouse carpark, which was cluttered with an unusual number of cars for a weekday.

From where the car stopped, the club seemed to consist of the neat clubhouse and, away to our left, the Skeet layouts beyond a stretch of grass and a bed of flowering heathers. But I knew that most of the facilities lay where the water seemed to begin, on a broad stretch of level ground below the drop of an embankment which bisected the site. The top of the tower showed above the clubhouse roof.

I could see uniformed officers conducting a meticulous search over by the three Skeet layouts, but a group beside a nearby car was in deep discussion. They were uniformly dressed in trousers and white shirts, complete with collars and ties but each with a jacket slung over one arm in deference to the heat of the day. An anticyclone had settled over Scotland a few days earlier and we were enjoying – or hating, according to taste – a rare heatwave.

'Do not say anything until I speak to you,' Mr Munro

whispered. He sounded more mischievous than I had ever known him to be.

As we got out of the car, leaving Sam to sulk on his own, they glanced at me with masculine interest and then, judging me to be without either importance or appeal, looked away. No woman likes to feel uninteresting. It was as humiliating as being ignored by a sex maniac. I could have kicked myself for not being firmer about going home to change, or Mr Munro for not heeding me.

The tallest man of the group detached himself, came over and shook hands with Mr Munro.

'Well, Gordon,' Mr Munro said. 'What is this help you're looking for?'

Gordon, whoever he might be, looked surprised. 'There was no need to come yourself, Hamish,' he said. 'We have a suspicious death here. Some of our officers go in for this clay pigeon shooting lark, but only at a lowly level with manually operated traps. We needed somebody who knows about these fancy gadgets.'

'It was quiet in the office. Show me the problem,' Mr Munro said. 'We'll see whether I can't be of any help.'

Gordon, who I soon gathered was Superintendent McHarg, hesitated and then, being out-ranked, he shrugged and led the way towards the Skeet layouts. I tagged along. The Superintendent had a definite Glasgow accent, but it was obvious that the two men not only knew but tolerated each other. I remembered then that a Hebridean, when he thinks of civilisation, turns his mind first to Inverness and then to Glasgow. The Glaswegian, therefore, despite being poles away in accent and attitude, becomes a sort of honorary Highlander.

A path had been marked out and we stayed strictly between the tapes. It led past the bed of heathers and a plastic bin set to receive spent cartridges, then right-handed round the first safety wall to the nearest of the three Skeet layouts. A semicircle of slabs set into the grass demarked the seven 'stations' from which a shooter would tackle the birds which would be sent across his front from the two trap-houses, but our path led along the wall to the end trap-house.

'Ah,' said Mr Munro knowingly. 'Skeet.' Mr McHarg looked at him sharply but I almost gave my pupil a pat on the back.

Near Station Seven, the outline of a human figure had been marked out with more tape, the feet towards the nearby trap-house. There was nothing to indicate whether the figure had been lying on its back or its face but, if the latter, its left hand would have been close to a twelve-bore over-under shotgun which still lay within its own tapes on the grass. An opened box of the club's standard twelve-bore cartridges, marked as loaded with No. 7 shot, stood nearby. An electric lead snaked over the grass.

'The postman found him this morning,' McHarg said. 'He needed a signature for a postal packet and he got no answer at the dwelling which is incorporated into the clubhouse, so he took a look around. The man was lying on his back with a wound across his forehead which had fractured the skull. The postman says that the dead man's name was Tullos and that he was the steward of the club and the regular occupant of the house. We can't count that as a formal identification, but it'll do for the moment.

'Superficially, it looks like an accident. The man could have come out of the house to do some solitary practising at this . . .'

'Skeet,' Mr Munro repeated. 'It is an old Scandinavian word, meaning to shoot.' Evidently, he was enjoying himself.

'Thank you. I suppose that's possible – for a man to work the machinery for himself?'

I was behind the backs of the group and being completely ignored. I saw Mr Munro seek my eye and I nodded. 'Perfectly possible,' he said.

'Well, then. For some reason the mechanism of that . . . machine failed to function.'

21

'You call it a trap,' Mr Munro said loftily. If he was tempted to go on and explain why a trap was so called, he refrained.

'I did know that,' McHarg snapped. 'I just forgot for the moment. The trap seems to be working perfectly now. But a trace of blood was found on the edge of the arm. The supposition is that he put his head in through the wee door to see what was wrong, and that the mechanism chose that moment to right itself. There is an arm with a thin edge which we think might fit the wound.'

The Chief Superintendent was still watching me covertly. I drew a cross on my forehead and he picked me up immediately. 'Did the wound run across the man's forehead,' he asked, 'or up and down?'

Superintendent McHarg looked surprised and impressed. 'You've put your finger on the problem,' he said. 'It ran parallel to the eyebrows, just the way you'd expect. But we've tried it – with the electricity turned off,' he added quickly. 'The little door where the clay pigeons come out is wider than it is high. A man can put his head inside, but not straight in. He has to twist it sideways. The way the trap is at the moment, if he had been struck by the arm he could not have been struck the way he was. You follow me?'

'You make it very clear,' Mr Munro said. 'Of course, there are traps incorporating tilting and swivelling movements . . .'

'That's what we thought,' McHarg said. 'But whatever we do with the controls of this one, it just throws another clay pigeon. My men have been dodging the damned things for half the morning.'

I had been shaking my head. The Chief Superintendent pretended to glance in through the opening. 'Not this one,' he said.

'That, if you'll forgive the expression, seems to knock the accident theory on the head,' Mr McHarg said. There were sycophantic snickers from the two minions who were still attached to the group.

'It would seem so,' Mr Munro said.

'It's a pity our first man got here after the dew was off the grass. The ground's too baked and it's been too much walked on to hold any useful impressions. The postman moved the dead man before he realised that he was in the presence of death. The pathologist may be able to tell us if the man was moved after death.'

Mr Munro sucked in his cheeks. 'But not if he was moved immediately.'

'Probably not. Perhaps Forensics will be able to help.' Superintendent McHarg seemed to be speaking to himself rather than to his colleagues, thinking aloud. 'My impression – and it's no more than that – is that the body was lying where it fell, allowing for any disturbance by the postman. I had some infra-red photographs taken along with the others, and they sometimes show something new. Unless and until they do, I think we make a provisional assumption that he was killed here. He came out early to get in some practice at – what did you call it? – at Skeet . . .'

While they spoke, I had taken a good look at the gun, which was lying, open as a gun should be when not in use, just beyond the tape marking the permitted path. It was a good-quality over-under with exchangeable chokes internally fitted at the muzzles. The ends of the chokes were identified by transverse notches, but makers are not uniform in their systems of marking – in other words, a single notch may signify the tightest or the most open choke. I sometimes carry a brass key-ring which incorporates a simple choke-gauge, but not when ratting.

There was another simple if approximate check. I had been shooting rabbits with Ronnie the previous evening and I still had a fired twenty-bore cartridge in my pocket. I stooped down. Nobody was paying any attention to me. The cartridge fitted very tightly into one muzzle while in the other it would only slide as far as the beginning of its metal base. I straightened up and shook my head at the Chief Superintendent.

'I'm afraid you're wrong, Gordon,' Mr Munro interrupted.

Mr McHarg broke off, looking peeved. 'Why would that be?'

'Perhaps Miss Calder had better explain.'

TWO

From his tone, you would never have guessed that Chief Superintendent Munro was as much in the dark as the others. 'This is my expert,' he added blandly. 'Her father, my usual consultant, is abroad just now, so Miss Calder has kindly agreed to deputise for him.' He waited, smiling his rare and lop-sided smile, enjoying the looks on their faces.

I spoke up quickly before one of them could point out that I was 'only a girl'. At the same time I shot Mr Munro a dirty look. In having his little fun, he had pushed me in at the deep end.

'That gun has chokes which can be exchanged,' I said. 'Chokes are the constrictions at the muzzles which determine the concentration and therefore the range of the shot pattern.' I paused, but none of them admitted to being baffled so I pressed on. 'It seems to be fitted with full and three-quarter chokes at the moment. But Skeet is a fast sport and the birds are taken close; you want the most open patterns you can get – true and improved cylinders, or improved and quarter-choke. Mr Tullos was a good shot and an approved CPSA coach—'

'That would be the Clay Pigeon Shooting Association,' Mr Munro said kindly, passing on one of my own fragments of information. It came back to me that Mr Munro's division had never had a proper Criminal Investigation Branch but had had to depend on Edinburgh in the event of any crime which could possibly be considered serious. This had always rankled with the Chief Superintendent, who

25

was now revelling in this golden chance to stick his oar into a major case outside his own territory.

'The idea of an accident sounds perfectly possible,' I said. 'Sometimes an ejected cartridge flips through the opening and it was Mr Tullos's job to gather them up. He could have forgotten that the trap was still live. But that trap doesn't tilt. If you say that he couldn't have put his head inside without laying it over, I'll believe you. I just don't believe that he came out to shoot Skeet. No way would he have come to the Skeet layout with those chokes in his gun,' I finished. 'If we can go into the buildings, I can show you what I mean.'

Superintendent McHarg looked at me as though uncertain whether to ask for more details or to give me a sweetie and a pat on the head and to send me home. 'Do you shoot?' he asked doubtfully.

'All my life,' I said. 'I've shot Skeet here at least fifty times. You'll find my name on the ladies' trophy in the clubhouse. Do you mind telling me what Mr Tullos was wearing?'

'Shirt and trousers,' somebody said.

'If he'd intended to shoot, he'd have been wearing another layer, probably a Skeet vest – one of those waistcoat things with big pockets,' I explained. 'You need two layers of clothing to absorb the friction of recoil between them. And he was very meticulous about wearing ear-protectors and shatterproof glasses.'

'He had ear-muffs on,' one of the minions said. 'There were some odd-looking glasses in the pocket of his shirt.'

'In Skeet,' I said, 'some of the birds are taken approaching and quite close. And bits of clay can hurt when they hit you on the head, so for Skeet he usually wore one of the club's blue caps, like a baseball cap.'

The tall man – he topped even Mr Munro by at least an inch – looked almost relieved. 'There was nothing like that. Have they finished in the house?' he asked one of his subordinates. The man bustled away.

'There's another thing,' I said. 'It's possible to shoot by yourself, holding the remote control in your left hand, but it's difficult. The club has an acoustic release, which sends the bird when you call, by responding to the sound of your voice. If he'd planned to shoot Skeet on his own, he'd have plugged it in. Do you want me to look and see if it's been plugged in somewhere else?'

'Later, perhaps. We haven't been able to make contact with any of the club officials,' he said to Mr Munro. 'Except the deceased, of course.'

'The secretary is Mr Glencorse,' I said. 'He's an engineer, but I don't know where he works. Sir Peter Hay is the chairman.'

Mr Munro tutted. 'I wish you'd said that sooner. When Wallace James said that you had gone with your uncle, I telephoned Sir Peter to ask where you were likely to be found.'

Superintendent McHarg wasted no words on what might have been. 'Get on the radio,' he told the other hanger-on. 'Get a message to Sir Peter Hay. Ask him to meet you at wherever they've taken the body, to make formal identification. Then, if he can make himself available, he'd better come out here.' He switched his eyes, which were grey and rather macho, to me. 'Can you describe Mr Tullos?'

'Easily,' I said. 'He is or was about three inches taller than me, middle-aged going on elderly, rather thin and totally bald. He had a pointed nose, rather rat-like but not in a nasty sort of way. And he walked with a limp.'

He nodded. 'That sounds very much like the dead man. What do you know about him?'

When I came to think about it, Mr Tullos had been a background figure, somebody to be contended with rather than engaged in conversation. I gathered up the fragments that I knew. 'He was in the police at one time,' I said.

Mr McHarg stared at me. 'Not in this force, surely?'

'No, not here. His accent was local but I think he served in Glasgow. From what he said, his limp was the

27

result of an injury while on duty, but I wouldn't put it past him to have been spinning a tale. He was pensioned and he worked abroad for a while before he took the job here. I don't believe he was paid much of a salary – I've heard him grumble about it – but he lived rent-free in the house, earned fees for coaching, and I think there were a few perks. In return he looked after the place, took the money for cartridges and day memberships and so on, arranged competitions at weekends and did everything down to serving light meals, filling the coffee machines and putting new paper in the shunkies. Anything you wanted, you asked Mr Tullos for it, and, if he liked you, you got it. Not many people got what they wanted.'

'He was unpopular?'

I thought carefully before I answered. 'I don't want to exaggerate,' I said. 'I can't think of anybody who liked him much but I don't know of anybody who hated him – certainly not enough to kill him. He was a cantankerous old cuss and more interested in the place itself than in its members. For instance, he tried to get dogs banned although many of the members like to shoot with their dogs beside them. It's the best way to teach a dog that a shot doesn't necessarily mean a retrieve. He was a good shot but, frankly, he wasn't a good teacher.' The men were listening raptly. I paused and tried to think of some more goodies for them. 'When he arranged competitions at the weekends, which were usually English Sporting—'

'That is what you would call FITASC,' Mr Munro put in. 'Springing grouse and suchlike.'

Evidently my words of wisdom had fallen short. FITASC resembles English Sporting and yet is quite different and much more difficult. '—he used to enter and win more than his fair share,' I said firmly. 'He waited until he saw who had turned up, and if there was nobody there who was good at . . .' I paused. For the moment I could think of nothing but springing teal and driven grouse, either of which would have exposed Mr Munro's total ignorance of

28

the subject. '... any particular bird,' I resumed, 'that's what we got. And, which was worse, when he won he got cocky about it.'

'Were there any times when tempers flared?'

'Off and on,' I said. 'He could be pleasant when he wanted to, but he had a rough edge to his tongue and some of the members ... Well, it isn't only the gentry who have the money these days. Some of the members and visitors work on the oil-rigs or in industry. I've heard some slanging-matches and a lot of language my mother didn't appreciate.'

'Your mother?' The Superintendent's more chauvinist preconceptions were being outraged.

'We have a family membership and she sometimes comes along for the fun of it. She's quite good at Sporting although she isn't a serious competitor, like some. Clay shooters take it more seriously than game shots,' I explained. 'A sociable man who enjoys the country scene may go shooting game or pests and come clay-busting now and again to keep his eye in. Regular clay shooters are a different breed. They get into it because they enjoy shooting, but also because they're competitive by nature. Some of them are only out for fun and practice, but there's a percentage who're fighting their way to the top or to stay there, or who pay for their shooting with what they can win at competitions. Those ones can have very short fuses.'

'Punch-ups?' the Superintendent asked eagerly.

'Very, very rare,' I said. 'Raised voices are permissible, raised fists are not. Violence is dangerous when there are guns around, so a man can get himself banned that way. And remember that these aren't street-corner rowdies. These are men who are getting rid of all their aggression in competitiveness and noise.' I almost added that violence is the prerogative of men without any better outlet, but doubted whether he would accept such philosophising from me. The Superintendent was undoubtedly sexist. Besides, I knew that I was talking too much.

29

The first minion came back then, to say that the search of the house had been finished. Superintendent McHarg began to move in that direction.

'It is time that I was going back to my desk,' Mr Munro said. 'Don't hesitate to call on me again, Gordon, if I can be of any help.'

'Here,' I said, 'what about me? How do I get home?'

'I'm sure that Superintendent McHarg can arrange transport for you. Do you want to keep my expert for any longer, Gordon?'

Mr McHarg, I was sure, would have liked to tell him to take his expert away and lose her, or worse, but I was the nearest that he had to a witness with local knowledge. 'Leave Miss Calder with me,' he said. 'I'll see that she gets home. And . . . thank you, Hamish.'

The last words came out with all the eager spontaneity of somebody passing a lump of coke. Chief Superintendent Munro had been enjoying his moment of triumph with a little too much relish. But he was escorted to his car with great courtesy and the two men sketched salutes. I remembered to recover Sam from the floor at the back. Mr Munro winked at me and then his driver swept him away.

Superintendent McHarg stood looking after the car for a few seconds through narrowed eyes. Mr Munro might be an old friend and hold a superior rank, but he belonged to the uniformed branch, always considered to be an inferior calling by those in plain clothes. The patronage had rankled.

'Right, young woman,' he said. 'Come with me and don't let that dog wander one inch off the path.' He stalked towards the club buildings. With the departure of my patron, politeness had become superfluous.

I could have matched his rudeness – Mum says that I have inherited Dad's hair-trigger – but I was becoming interested and had no wish to be packed off home like a naughty child. I put Sam on his lead and followed, trotting to keep up.

First Minion fell in beside me. 'Sergeant Fellowes,' he said helpfully.

'Deborah Calder,' I replied. I put out my hand. He hesitated and then shook it without slowing down. I thought that he seemed rather surprised, as though such courtesies were not the norm between officers and witnesses. Later, I realised that he had been checking to see that my hand was clean enough to shake. With my clothes still dusty from ratting, I could hardly blame him.

The Superintendent led us to a door in the gable of the club buildings. I attached Sam to a substantial boot-scraper and we went inside.

'Without touching anything,' the Superintendent said, 'point out whatever you wanted to show me.'

Mr Tullos, or somebody else, had kept the small house in meticulous order, although there were now signs of a search and a dusting of grey fingerprint powder on doorhandles and window latches. The living-room was barely large enough for a suite and a television set. The three-quarter bed in the main bedroom had been remade since Mr Tullos last occupied it. There was a spare bedroom so tiny that it accommodated only a pair of bunk-beds, one above the other. The kitchen, with dining alcove, was well equipped and tidy. The whole place was as compact as a caravan. Everything was on show except what I was looking for.

'We'd better try the office,' I said.

The Superintendent frowned. 'Is there an office?' he asked the Sergeant.

An expression of concern flitted across the Sergeant's face. 'I don't think we could have missed a whole office, sir,' he said.

Mr McHarg looked at him as though one of his turds had answered him back. 'I know that you can't help being funny,' he said, 'but don't be funny on purpose.'

Sergeant Fellowes waited impassively.

I had only been into the office from the clubhouse

31

side, but I was sure that I had seen a door to the house. There was a door at the end of a short leg off the corridor which served as a hallway in the house and this seemed to be aligned more or less with the one off the clubroom. 'Do you have Mr Tullos's keys?' I asked the Superintendent.

'I have them,' said Sergeant Fellowes. He pulled out a ring of keys and, after some fumbling with the security lock, opened the door. It swung open heavily to reveal another short corridor with a door each side and the clubroom door beyond. The Superintendent made a sound of disgust.

The Sergeant looked for a moment like a small boy caught stealing apples. 'I'll be damned,' he said. 'I thought that this was the same door that you see from the clubroom.'

'From outside, you wouldn't know it was there,' I said consolingly. 'No windows.'

The door on our right – to the front of the building – was the store. I showed them the racked cartons of cartridges, clay pigeons and miscellaneous gear. Opposite was the office, a narrow room lit only by a heavily barred rooflight and a fluorescent tube. There was a desk littered with papers, several four-drawer filing cabinets and a large gun-safe.

'Fetch Jimmy Johnson,' Mr McHarg said. 'We don't touch anything until he's checked for prints.'

The Sergeant hurried out.

On a corner of the desk there was a plastic case with compartments for six choke-tubes and a key. The first two chokes from the left were missing.

A stout man of around fifty in an unsuitable tweed suit came in carrying an attaché case and looked expectantly at the Superintendent.

'Could he check these first?' I asked. 'I doubt if anybody's managed to leave a print inside one of them, but it's possible. You can tell the chokes apart by feel.'

Mr McHarg nodded.

The stout man blew some grey powder into each of the chokes, shook his head, wiped them clean and replaced them in the case in their proper order. Without waiting for further instructions he moved on to the handles of the gun-safe, the door and the various drawers.

The Superintendent, meanwhile, had been studying the diary which lay open on the desk. 'Nothing after midday on Monday – yesterday – when he seems to have had an appointment with a B. Torry at twelve noon. Nothing today. H. Noble seems to have an appointment on Friday for ES. What would that be?'

'English Sporting, I should think. It's the discipline that game shooters tend to go for. Harry Noble has a dud shoulder. He has to shoot one-handed and he isn't very good at it. He needs coaching and he probably decided to pay for it.'

'Ah. Against yesterday it also says GC. Any ideas?'

I wasted some seconds in profitless thought. 'Gun Club,' I suggested. 'But that doesn't mean anything. Golf Course? There's a Gertrude Cowan among the members. Or there may be a man with those initials.'

The Superintendent flicked over the pages of the diary with a letter opener. 'GC turns up every second Monday,' he said.

'Probably somebody with a regular appointment for coaching,' I suggested. 'The club's supposed to be shut on Mondays, to give the steward some time off, but Mr Tullos never minded opening up if there was something in it for himself. Or Gun Cleaning – he may have liked a reminder to give his own and the club's guns a going-over once a fortnight.'

I tried the choke-tubes from the case with my twenty-bore cartridge and found that they varied between a tight fit round the cartridge's metal base to a loose fit which was only stopped by the rim.

'So?' the Superintendent said impatiently.

'As I thought,' I said. Even to myself I sounded like Sherlock Holmes at his most pompous. 'If these chokes belong to the gun outside, then, as near as I can tell by a rough check, the gun's fitted with full and three-quarter chokes. If he was planning to shoot Skeet, he'd have used the two from the other end of the row. For Sporting, maybe the two middle ones of the four still in the case, unless he was tackling very high birds. The chokes in the gun are for the going-away disciplines. They're a rather different game. People tend to specialise in them or avoid them. Mr Tullos was an all-rounder but he preferred Skeet and Sporting.'

'Hm,' said the Superintendent. It was impossible to tell whether he had understood a single word. He frowned at me for most of a minute. 'Drawing conclusions is my responsibility,' he said at last. 'But if I asked you what you concluded . . . ?'

'The gun out there looks very much like Mr Tullos's own gun,' I said. 'He was very careful with it, so he'd certainly have taken the chokes out and oiled the threads before putting it away. It's just possible that somebody came up here wanting to be coached in one of the going-away disciplines, and that this was the only gun which fitted him. I doubt that, because Mr Tullos was of average build and there are several club guns in that safe. My best guesses would be either that somebody swatted him with something like the blunt edge of a kitchen cleaver, tried to make it look like an accident but made a bad guess about the chokes; or that somebody challenged him at Down the Line or Ball-trap, with money on it, and then there was a quarrel with a similar result; or else that he saw something threatening outside – vandals, perhaps, or an old enemy – and he took the gun out with him for his own protection.'

'If he was hurrying outside to meet some threat, would he hang about putting chokes into his gun?'

'Nobody who cared for his gun would use it with internal chokes missing,' I said. 'The threads would be ruined.'

I probably sounded shocked. The Superintendent looked amused for a moment, but then his frown came back. 'We'll have to treat this as a murder inquiry,' he said.

'Sergeant, take Miss Calder somewhere quiet and get a full statement.'

'Then can I go home?' I asked.

He shook his head. 'We'd be grateful if you waited a little longer. There will be more questions.'

Sergeant Fellowes led me back the way we had come. Somebody had given Sam a plastic box filled with water.

'You?' I asked.

He nodded. 'It's hot in the sun. And he can't leave off his fur coat as you can.'

'Thank you,' I said, picking up the lead. 'That was very considerate. But I don't have a fur coat.'

'I'm a considerate sort of person,' he said, 'but on police pay you won't get one from me.' I looked at him suddenly and caught the smile in his eyes. Instantly, he stopped being one of a mass of faceless figures in an authoritarian team and became an individual. At the same moment I knew, in the intangible way that such knowledge comes, that despite my unflattering rig and probably rather pedantic manner something in him was responding to something in me.

'Did I drop you in it?' I asked.

'You did. But I was doomed to be dropped in it anyway. Better sooner than later.'

He proved his considerateness by finding us a seat on a bench in the shade of the building and then going to fetch us each a plastic cup of coffee from the machine in the clubroom. I watched the searchers scouring the ground without any of us having the faintest idea what they were looking for. The Sergeant took a seat beside me, put his coffee down carefully on his other side and produced a notebook.

'Before we begin,' I said, 'tell me what we're talking about. Was he killed last night or this morning?'

The Sergeant shrugged and then made a face. 'Either,' he said. 'The police surgeon suggested late yesterday evening, but rigor and body temperature are very variable and defence counsel always knows it, so the doctors are always careful to allow themselves a lot of margin. In this case it's not as big a margin as it sounds, because the sun doesn't go down for very long, this far north and at this time of year. I suppose you could shoot until about eleven p.m. and then resume around three in the morning?'

'Something like that,' I said.

'Both well within the bracket. The pathologist may be able to be more exact if we happen to find out—' The Sergeant chopped his sentence off.

'When he ate his last meal?' I finished for him. 'It's all right. I'm quite tough and I've been involved in these things before.'

'I'll remember. Was Mr Tullos usually early to bed and early to rise? Or the reverse?'

I was about to say that I wouldn't know because I'd never gone to bed with him. But when I thought about it I realised how imperceptibly knowledge can accumulate. The late Mr Tullos had never discussed his sleeping arrangements with me, but a hundred fragments of overheard conversations all came together to present me with a complete picture. 'I don't think that he was a long sleeper,' I said. 'From what I've heard, a very few hours at night were enough for him and he sometimes made up by cat-napping during the day. But you'd better ask one of the members who knew him better.'

There was a pause of a few seconds while the Sergeant finished writing. 'That was going to be my next question,' he said. 'Which members knew him well?'

'I couldn't tell you,' I said. 'He was on rather scratchy terms with all of them. He was one of those men who think that a joke is an insult. You can't always tell whether it's meant affectionately or not. You know what I mean?'

'I know exactly what you mean,' the Sergeant said.

'You could try Harry Noble. Mr Tullos seemed to be more patient with him than with anybody else. Harry tries very hard, but he's only got one arm. I mean,' I corrected myself, 'he's got both arms, but—'

'They're both on the same side?'

'—but he can't lift his left arm because of some old injury. You ass!' I added. But I snorted with laughter and nearly spilled my coffee. In fact, I was secretly delighted to discover that, like myself, the Sergeant had a sense of the ridiculous constantly trying to escape. 'So Mr Tullos spent hours helping Harry learn to shoot one-handed, which is difficult because it's usually the left hand which does most of the aiming.'

The Sergeant was looking slightly ashamed and trying to pretend that he had never let the mask slip. 'We'll try your Mr Noble,' he said.

He flipped a page in his notebook and looked at the blank paper thoughtfully. I looked at him, seeing him now as a male person rather than as a policeman. He was, I noticed, cast in the square and sandy-haired southern Scottish style which is in contrast to the lean and dark Celtic Highlanders. It is a style which I have always thought pleasant rather than handsome, but I liked it. Handsome men, like beautiful women, get brainwashed by undeserved attention and stop being proper people. He had a short nose, firm jaw and eyes which I knew were ready to smile. But at the moment those eyes were looking past me.

'Next question. . . . Who's this?'

'Easy one,' I said. 'That's the club chairman.' Sir Peter Hay was getting out of one of his battered Land-rovers. His mop of grey hair was even more tangled than usual and he was wearing the least presentable of his many kilts. When I was young, I thought that he must be nearly a hundred years old; but now I realised that he was a sprightly seventy, so perhaps he had mastered the trick of growing younger. He was my godfather, a close friend of my parents and the best-intentioned person I ever met. I would have died for him.

THREE

Sir Peter ambled across the carpark and stopped in front of us. 'Deborah, my dear child,' he said, 'how did you get dragged into this?' He is one of the many people who still speak to me as though I were ten years old, but from him, perhaps because of his age, it seems acceptable. All the same, it was a good moment to remind him that I am now adult.

'They wanted my advice,' I said. 'This is Sergeant Fellowes. Sir Peter Hay.'

Sir Peter nodded politely. 'I identified the – er – the body. It was Herbert Tullos. He was our steward for the past four or five years.'

The Sergeant, no less polite, had risen to his feet at Sir Peter's approach. 'Do you know where he was before that, sir?'

'I still have his application on file. I'll dig it out for you. He'd just retired from a desk job with one of the oil companies. He was with the police before that and I seem to remember that he'd worked abroad in between.'

The Sergeant finished jotting in his book. 'The Super will want to know that,' he said, 'and anything else you can remember. He'll probably want to see you, Sir Peter. Will you wait?'

'Of course, my boy, of course.' Sir Peter sat down beside me and waited, fussing with Sam who, like most dogs, adored him, until the Sergeant had vanished into the building. 'I trust that they're treating you with respect,' he said to me in his rather fluting voice.

38

'The Sergeant's been very considerate,' I said. Sir Peter always seemed to know absolutely everybody, certainly up to and including the Secretary of State, probably the Prime Minister and quite possibly God; and when he was on the warpath he sometimes pulled the most astonishing strings. He would have been quite capable of using all those resources if I had mentioned that one of the policemen had been curt with me. I decided not to ask for the Superintendent's head on a plate just yet. Later would do.

'That's all right, then. Can't think what they wanted you for, though.'

'General information on clay-busting,' I said. 'They couldn't find anybody else in a hurry.'

He smiled with his eyes. 'In other words, they wanted your father?'

'Well, yes.'

'I can't think of much that he could tell them that you couldn't,' he said kindly.

'Thank you,' I said. 'But I have a nasty feeling that I've already missed something that he'd have spotted.'

'I doubt it.' He smiled again for a moment and then looked serious. 'All I know for the moment is that Herbert Tullos has been killed. I could see for myself that he'd had a whack across the nut. Didn't look accidental to me. Do they suspect what they call foul play?'

'It looks very like it. Somebody made a rather poor job of trying to pass it off as an accident.'

The return of Sergeant Fellowes cut short his questions. The Sergeant was alone and carrying a tray with more coffee and a stack of sandwiches. 'The men's "refreshments" arrived,' he said. 'Why should we go hungry? The Superintendent can't get away. He apologises and asks me to get both of your statements.'

He sat down on my other side. As 'pig in the middle' I seemed to be elected to hold the tray.

'You were right, my dear, he is considerate. I want to

39

know what's going on,' Sir Peter said plaintively. He was clearly upset, but not too upset to help himself to one of the egg, meat and tomato sandwiches.

'Of course, Sir Peter,' the Sergeant said. 'Herbert Tullos was found dead this morning, by the postman. As far as I know, no significant information has turned up yet, but Miss Calder was able to . . . to help our understanding of the case. I was about to take her statement. Perhaps if we heard her out together . . . ?'

'Of course.'

As lucidly as I could, I dictated a statement covering what I had seen and the reasons why Mr Tullos could not have died an accidental death. I held a sandwich as I spoke, more to reserve it for myself than in the hope of taking a bite out of it. The other sandwiches vanished.

The Sergeant seemed to have the knack of eating while writing clearly and rapidly in his notebook. When my statement was finished, he swallowed the last of the last sandwich. 'That seems clear,' he said. 'I'll get it transcribed for your signature.'

'Just a moment,' Sir Peter broke in. 'Those may be the facts. But I've seen this young lady and her father at work. Deborah, can you draw any inferences out of all this?'

I waited until I had managed to swallow the remains of my only sandwich. 'Just this,' I said. 'If I'm right and there was a criminal—'

'A murderer,' Sir Peter said, sadly. 'I'm afraid that we have to face up to that.'

'Or somebody trying to cover up an accident or a suicide,' I pointed out. They looked at me in puzzlement but made no comment. 'In the event,' I said, 'he wasn't one of the hot-shots. Nobody who was really into shotguns would make a mistake about chokes. Any fool knows that you can tell the difference between tight and open chokes by pushing in a fingertip. And if he was a regular shooter here, he'd know that there were better trap-houses for faking a convincing accident. All the trap-houses have at least two openings.' I explained to the Sergeant. 'You don't want anybody trying to load the magazine through the front where the throwing-arm comes round, or reaching in to pick up an ejected cartridge which has found its way inside. So you only have a little opening at the front and there's a bigger door in the back or side. The direction of throw at Skeet is fixed, so the opening can be comparatively small. But some of the trap-houses have larger openings at the front or top, where a head could be put inside if its owner was rash enough or tired of life. Anybody who knew anything would have gone to one of those.'

'He might not have the strength or the stomach to carry a dead body around,' the Sergeant said. 'And it isn't easy to arrange a body and its clothing to look as though it lies where it fell. He couldn't count on the postman who found the body to move it around and then to admit having done so.'

'Unless the postman did it,' I said.

My remark was made in all seriousness and seemed perfectly logical to me. There was, after all, one person who could be sure that the postman would move the body and own up to it. But Sir Peter gave me the reproving glance which he usually reserves for occasions when I have been frivolous. 'You make me sorry that I asked the question,' he said.

'It was a reasonable suggestion,' the Sergeant said. 'We had to consider it. In fact, we haven't written it off entirely. But if the postie had anything to do with it, he should be on the stage – with his ability to portray shock and distress.'

Sir Peter shrugged. 'As to the murderer being unfamiliar with clay pigeon shooting,' he said to me, 'you may be right, or you may not. On this occasion, I think that you've jumped to a premature conclusion and overlooked another explanation of at least equal likelihood.' He looked at the Sergeant. 'I need hardly ask whether you'll be enquiring whether any of the dwellers in that overpriced extravaganza further along the waterside saw anything.'

41

'Men are making door-to-door enquiries already.'

'Time enough to theorise when you have the answers. For the moment, I suggest that you discount our young friend's last assumptions.' He looked at the view before us, limited though it was, and half smiled. 'And now,' he said, switching to what I always think of as his chairman's manner, 'suppose you tell me when we're likely to regain the use of the club's facilities.'

'Knowing how the Super usually works,' Sergeant Fellowes said, 'my best guess would be that he'll use the clubhouse as a temporary Incident Room until a complete search has been finished, perhaps late tomorrow. After that, he'll prefer to be near a computer facility. He'll move everything to a more permanent base at Headquarters. That's assuming that we don't make a quick arrest.'

'Then for tonight and tomorrow night,' Sir Peter said firmly, 'I'm holding you responsible for the security of premises and equipment. We'll take the keys back from you on Thursday.'

'You've had trouble here?' the Sergeant asked quickly.

'Not often, while Herbert Tullos was in residence. He was more than able to deal with the occasional young vandals. But he only had to take a holiday, or go away with a team, and the youngsters from next door would invade the place. That's why we have steel doors on all the trap-houses. The kids wouldn't bother in the normal course of events, but some parents are anti-gun and the manager at the Leisure Complex eggs them on. Not directly, but you know how youngsters can take a hint from their seniors.'

'The Leisure Complex resents the Gun Club?'

'Not to the extent of knocking off our officials,' Sir Peter said, 'but, yes. It's the noise that they complain about, mostly, although you can hardly hear the shooting from there unless the wind's from a direction which only happens about twice a year. But they try to make propaganda about almost anything else. About danger, which is a nonsense – spent shot pattering down from a height never hurt anybody. About ethics, which is frankly preposterous. And about disturbance to wildfowl and a risk of lead poisoning, both of which are quite untrue.

'They appealed to both local authorities in the hope of getting our planning permission revoked, but we were here first and they knew it before they adopted their site. The area was zoned for recreation, you see. In point of fact, we objected before they were granted planning permission, on the grounds that there would be conflict, but the Region sent a delegation to observe and it was decided that the noise nuisance was small and that there was no danger. They gave them a grant towards creating an embankment between the two sites, for noise attenuation, and left us to learn to live with each other – which, in fact, we do quite well. Some of the timeshare residents shoot here and some of our members also golf at the Country Club. It's only their management that stirs it up. There have been offers to buy us out, but so far the committee has resisted.'

'Was Mr Tullos involved in those discussions?' the Sergeant asked.

'He was on the committee. He was adamantly opposed to any sell-out. And so was I.'

'Well . . .' The Sergeant seemed uncertain whether to follow that line further. 'Well, that's one possible area of friction,' he said at last. 'Can you think of any others?'

Sir Peter shook his head. 'You'd better ask Deborah – Miss Calder – about that. I didn't shoot here as often as I might have done, just once a month or so to keep my eye in. Could have done with more practice, really, but time's too precious to fritter away. I used to ring Mr Tullos up at weekends to find out what was on, and if there was a competition in Sporting, I'd try to get along. Never won anything – I'm a rotten shot. Don't know why they made me chairman.'

Sir Peter, as an energetic worker and a generous sponsor when help was needed, was on almost every committee and

43

board for miles around, but he could never understand why the willing horse was so overworked.

The Sergeant was looking at me in enquiry. 'I can't help much,' I said. 'He was a rather scratchy and abrasive character—'

'I never found him so,' Sir Peter said.

'Well, you wouldn't. You're you. And you're the chairman. I don't remember that he was worse with any one person than any other. For a bunch which included some tough characters, they were usually careful not to quarrel openly with ladies present. I think that that's why they sometimes resented my presence. Having to moderate their language when they missed,' I explained.

'They resented your presence,' Sir Peter said, 'because you're turning into a damned good shot. Diehard chauvinists don't like being beaten by a chit of a girl, especially in what they regard as a male preserve. Didn't you ever notice that your father was very selective about which competitions he'd enter you for? He wanted you to be accepted. So he left you among the spectators if he thought there was a risk that you'd beat somebody who'd take it amiss.'

It had never occurred to me that there was any logic behind Dad's autocratic selection of competitions for me to enter. I knew that I could shoot and that girls well-taught while young could be very good, but the idea that I was becoming a threat to male egos was new. I found that I had lost my voice.

Luckily, the Sergeant was speaking. He had taken a computer print-out from his pocket and was unfolding it. 'We found a list of members in the office. Between you, perhaps you could fill in some detail.'

'It won't help you very much,' Sir Peter said. 'For historical reasons, entry to full membership is restricted and expensive. Longstanding members remain members even when they've moved away or even gone abroad. But we let others shoot here for the price of a day-membership. They think of themselves as members, but they're not. And, of

44

course, they don't appear on any list. You may be able to identify some of them from the receipts book.'

The Sergeant insisted and we did our best, but it seemed that only about a dozen of the members on the list were still active. On the other hand, we were able to remember and describe about twenty regular visiting non-members and to put at least one name to most of them.

'Thank you,' the Sergeant said at last. 'If we find any more names among the receipts, we'll ask you again.'

'Whenever you like.' Sir Peter was frowning in thought. 'When your Superintendent removes the epicentre of this investigation to your Headquarters, will there still be somebody up here?'

'Yes. At least by day. Why?'

'The club can't operate without somebody on site, to take entries, sell cartridges, give coaching and generally look after the place. I was about to ask Miss Calder whether she'd take it on.'

'Me?'

'Just until we can find somebody permanent. Sam Pollinder might do it. He's on your list, Sergeant. He's a widower who's in the process of retiring from school-teaching and it's not an unattractive retirement position for a keen shot. But I don't think that he'd be available this week or next.'

'Well . . .' I said weakly. The sudden onrush of responsibility, just when I had thought myself to be a lady of leisure, took my breath away. And I had never really thought of myself as employable outside of the family business.

'Will you do it, my dear? Or are you too busy? The club's only open afternoons and evenings and it closes on Sunday evening and all day on Monday unless the steward decides otherwise. I'm sure that Hugh Glencorse, the Club Secretary, would come and lend a hand over the weekend and I'd look in whenever I could.'

'Well . . .' I said yet again.

Sir Peter sighed. He tried to run his fingers through

his tangle of hair but only got so far. 'The alternative would be to notify all members and regular visitors that the club's closed until further notice. And then I'd have to mobilise as many as I could get hold of, to come and move the traps into the store and make the whole shebang as vandal-proof as possible. And by the time we resumed, the casuals would have started going somewhere else and then the whole operation would lose its head of steam.'

I never could resist Sir Peter when he looked sad, any more than he could resist me when I conjured up a tear. With each other, we were a pair of cajoling fakers. Perhaps that is why we got along so well. 'I'm not too busy,' I said slowly. 'But what about nights? I wouldn't want to sleep here on my own.'

'No question of that,' he said hastily. 'We'll work something out. I haven't had time to think what, but something.'

'Well . . .' I said again.

'I hope you'll do it,' the Sergeant said suddenly. 'If the place keeps going it should make it much easier for us to contact the regular attenders among the non-members.'

I made a rather vague gesture of assent.

'That's splendid,' Sir Peter said briskly. 'And now, I must go. I'm due at a meeting in Edinburgh. I'll be late, but that can't be helped.'

I walked to the Land-rover with him. 'I'll let it be known that business will be as usual from Thursday midday,' he said. 'I'm grateful. And you won't find it a total loss. You'll get a small retainer, and you keep any coaching fees and the profit on cartridges and the re-sale of clays. Either Hugh or I will call in and give you a briefing.' He lowered his voice as we arrived at the battered vehicle. 'I think you've made a conquest there,' he said.

I wondered whether the astute old gentleman had tuned in to the vibrations which were passing between the Sergeant and myself. But when I caught sight of my reflection in one of the dusty windows, I looked like an urchin of indeterminate sex. 'You've got to be joking,' I said.

'He seemed almost as anxious as I was to have you about the place. Well, we shall see.'

'What shall we see?'

'We'll see whether he's the officer who comes to do duty here. I'll be in touch.'

He drove off, battering over the bumps, and I was alone again except for a small army of policemen. At least I supposed that I would be safe in such company.

Sergeant Fellowes was waiting.

'Could we take a walk around?' I asked him.

'To survey your new domain?' He glanced at his watch. 'I can be spared for a few more minutes. But we must stick to the paths.'

We left Sam behind and stuck to the paths. I knew exactly where I wanted to go. At each stand there was a plastic drum, acting as a bin for the collection of spent cartridges. The bins at the Skeet layouts were empty. I led the way towards the water.

A flight of steps led down a steep bank, and from their head I could look over the other layouts. A clay pigeon club can be squeezed into a remarkably small space, provided that all the members are to shoot the same stand at the same time. But the Pentland Gun Club had been laid out on the assumption that several disciplines might be shot simultaneously, and the requirements of safety – not only from shot but also from the clay pigeons themselves – had necessitated dispersal over perhaps a hundred acres.

To my left, not far from the noise attenuation banking which bounded the site, the going-away disciplines – Down the Line and Ball-trap – were placed. The rest of the site was patterned by a long maze of paths of quarry dust which threaded among the stands so that varied use of the dozen traps could present an infinite variation of birds. The layout had incorporated the already existing stands of trees; birds could be presented to simulate conditions on a pheasant or partridge drive.

I started at the southern end, the end furthest from

the Leisure Complex, where the more specialised traps of the FITASC layout were, and walked along looking in the empty bins.

'As a matter of interest,' asked the Sergeant, 'what are we looking for?'

'When he thought that business was over for the day,' I explained, 'Mr Tullos was very conscientious about picking up unbroken clays and collecting fired cartridges. If he had a late visitor, or an early one in the morning. . .' I left the sentence unfinished as I stopped at the fourth bin. This was set in a small terrace of the ubiquitous quarry dust, between two of the wire-mesh safety cages which were designed to prevent a gun from swinging beyond the limits of safety. A dozen or so spent cartridges lay in the bottom.

The Sergeant looked in and grunted. 'What do you deduce from this?' he enquired.

'Somebody's been here since Harry Noble. Harry only shoots twenty-bore, because of his disability. He has to have a gun which is light enough to be used one-handed. Let's go on,' I said. 'He or they may not have been shooting just the one stand.'

We walked on to the end, close to the long mound which had been raised to screen the Leisure Complex from noise, but the bins were empty. We turned and looked back over the layouts. The clubhouse and the Skeet walls were diminished by the distance.

'Would your men have been picking up unbroken clay pigeons?' I asked.

He shook his head. 'There were too many of them lying around and they didn't mean anything. We're not in the business of tidying up behind other bodies.'

'Those would be broken clays. I think you'll find that there were very few whole ones, other than any which your lads pumped out of the Skeet trap while trying to puzzle out how it worked. Maybe none, if he was a good shot. If there are any unbroken ones, they'll mean a hell of a lot.'

Considering that I was younger, unofficial and female, he took it well. 'All right, tell me.'

'Mr Tullos always picked up unbroken clays. The member or visitor pays so much per shot to cover the cost of his clays, but the unbroken ones are the steward's perk. You don't use them again in the automatic traps, because if one turns out to be cracked and breaks in the magazine it can jam the whole works; but they're all right in manual traps, so smaller, local clay clubs buy them at half-price. If you look, you'll see that most of the traps are sited so that the clays will land on grass or low ground-cover. So let's see which bird was being shot. If he was good, he broke most of them; but if he came here for coaching or for practice at the one which usually beats him, we may find almost as many clays as there were empty cartridges.'

The Sergeant nodded slowly, absorbing what was, I suppose, almost a foreign language to him. He looked vaguely around him. 'So where do we search?' he asked.

The pair of stands where we found the cartridges were usually used in conjunction with the high tower. 'Somewhere below the clubhouse,' I said.

'That area's already been searched, so we can't do any harm. Let's go and take a look.'

We walked along the grass below the clubhouse. I stopped and aligned myself. 'If he was shooting left-to-right crossers,' I said, 'they'd be here, and they aren't, so either he wasn't or he was a better shot than I'll ever be.'

'There aren't even any bits,' the Sergeant said.

'Bits come down all over the place. And a well-hit clay goes to dust.'

We moved on. Four clays lay on the grass and there was another which seemed to have broken on landing. One of the cages was in line with the tower. 'Driven pheasants,' I said. 'Somebody may have been preparing for next season.'

The Sergeant walked back to the bin and stood looking down at the cartridges in the bottom. I counted them.

There were eleven. 'If he only hit six out of eleven, he's mediocre,' I said. 'But he may not have fired at every bird. These are the same brand and shot size as the box which was beside the body. Not that that means anything. It's the commonest cartridge used around here.'

'We might get fingerprints off these,' he said.

I shrugged. 'I doubt it. They've been pressed tight against the wall of the chamber by gas pressure and then thrown out by the ejectors.'

'But somebody had to pick them up and put them in the bin.'

'Probably Mr Tullos,' I pointed out.

'Possibly – although not necessarily – true. But at least we should be able to connect them with a particular gun by the firing-pin marks.'

'And the marks of the ejectors and the breech-faces. Could I have a look at one of them?' I asked. 'I don't want to handle it. Pick it up on the end of a pencil or something.' He did as I asked and I looked carefully at the ejector-marks. 'Conventional double gun,' I said, 'not an automatic. An over-under.'

'Either you're guessing,' he said, 'or you're a witch.'

'Neither,' I said. 'The ejectors in a side-by-side go further round the circumference of the chamber. That's about all I can tell you without resorting to my father's equipment for microphotographs, and your lab can do that better than I can.'

'That's so.'

'If you were a gentleman instead of a policeman, you wouldn't be in such a tearing hurry to agree with me when I'm being modest. Have you finished with me now?' I asked.

He laughed and took another glance at his watch. 'The Super's having a briefing of section heads in a few minutes. I think that one of the big brass is coming. He'll want you to come in and do your party piece. After that, I'll run you home.'

'Is it all right if I take a wander round?' I asked. He looked doubtful. 'Outside the club boundaries,' I added.

'Why not?' he said. 'Could you be back in that seat outside the clubhouse in, say, half an hour?'

'Without fail.'

'Don't get lost. I wouldn't want that.' He smiled again, suddenly and warmly, and turned away.

FOUR

I collected Sam from his place by the seat and he danced to let me know that he was happy to be walking again, even at heel. We left the club grounds through the gate in the high fence where a very bored constable was doing guard duty and turned towards the Leisure Complex, walking on the broad grass verge.

The fence ended. The timeshare units were a quarter of a mile off, sprawling hard but luxurious as a sphinx might sprawl. Beyond was the Country Club with its swimming pool, tennis courts and stables. The immediate foreground had been grassed and planted with scatterings of shrubs and young trees which were already stretching frailly upward. Some day it would be full-blown parkland. A tractor was hauling a mowing-machine over the grass. Two ponies carrying girls were pretending to be frightened by it.

Sir Peter's apparently casual remark had set me thinking. When he seemed to be nattering at random he was usually most worth attention. I turned towards the water along the outside of the Gun Club fence. Although the ground was generally descending my path rose slightly because I was climbing the long mound which had been raised as a noise barrier or with safety in mind. If the latter, the result had been quite the opposite of the intention, because heads could now appear without warning above the embankment. This had necessitated an adjustment of the Down the Line stands and it was no longer safe to give the shooters a right-to-left crosser 'on report' at the Driven Grouse.

52

Another example of what was either thoughtlessness or a deliberate bad neighbour policy was that the mound had a flattened top, broadening out as it neared the waterside. This had created an attractive terrace, slightly hollowed and fringed with shrubs, from which anyone prepared to brave the midges and more than a few thorns could watch the dinghies sailing or the activities of the Gun Club. There was even a rough barbecue pit and a topless oil drum containing sundry empty tins and bottles.

I was interrupted by a distant fanfare on an unmusical car-horn. Looking round, I had a view of the Gun Club entrance. The uniformed constable seemed to be refusing admission to a disreputable Land-rover which was emitting a noise like a wounded buffalo, either in protest or in order to attract somebody's attention. Such behaviour was out of keeping with the shy and gentle Sir Peter, so I decided that some pressing emergency must have brought him back in search of me. I began to retrace my steps, calling Sam away from his search for non-existent rabbits along the embankment. No rabbit would set up home so close to regular gunfire.

The Land-rover, it turned out, was not Sir Peter's but the even older and more ramshackle one belonging to my uncle. Ronnie saw me coming and drove a few yards to meet me. I came to the driver's window.

'Are you ready for a lift home yet?' he asked.

'I can't leave,' I said. 'They want me to hang on. I'm promised a lift home when they've finished with me.'

'Sir Peter thought that'd be so. He told me to bring you a wee case. Just a dress and some things.'

'God bless him!' I said. 'He's a gentleman. You'd never have thought of a thing like that.'

'I'd have thought of it,' he protested. 'I might not've done it, but I'd have thought.'

Ronnie got out and I changed in the back of the Land-rover. A fairly suitable frock and almost matching shoes had been carefully packed, along with tights, a hairbrush and some make-up. I was pleased to find a container of those moist tissues which come in so useful when soap and water are unavailable, because I was quite sure that the club's toilets would be out of bounds.

'You didn't do this packing,' I said loudly. Ronnie would have stuffed a few of the wrong things into a plastic carrier bag.

'Sir Peter helped,' Ronnie's voice admitted from somewhere out in the road. 'He was in an awfu' rush to be off for his meeting. But he was feared I'd make a hash of it on my own,' he added indignantly.

I wiped the driver's seat with a tissue before climbing over into it and making use of the mirror. Ronnie sighed and tramped around the vehicle. When I felt presentable, I climbed down into the road. Sam sniffed at me in surprise. He was accustomed to me in both my guises but he had never seen me transformed from one to the other so quickly.

'I'll see you later,' I said to Ronnie. 'There's a pie in the freezer. Turn the oven on at about six o'clock, put the pie in at six-fifteen and if I'm not at home by seven take it out again. Leave some for me. You'll remember all that?'

'Aye.' He paused and goggled at me in the way that means he is anxious about something. 'You'll be all right on your own?'

'I won't be on my own,' I pointed out. 'I'll be in sight of about half the Lothian and Borders Constabulary. Our police may not be what they were, but I don't think they go in for gang-bangs yet.'

'Some o' they boggers, I'd not be so sure,' Ronnie said, but he turned the Land-rover and drove off.

I called Sam to heel and turned back towards the Gun Club. The constable on the gate, who had only managed a superior nod when I walked out, now saluted and his lips moved in what might have been an embryo whistle.

Feeling much restored in morale, I sat down to wait on the seat by the clubhouse wall. I was cooler in my cotton frock. Sunshine was all very well, but it was good to get back into the shade.

When Sergeant Fellowes came to fetch me a few minutes later, only the faintest flicker of surprise showed that he had noticed my transformation from a hoyden into a decorous young lady. He beckoned and then led the way. By some subtlety of body language, his back managed to convey a suggestion of apology for preceding me. He really was a gentleman, it said, despite being a policeman. Poor Sam was left to wait outside again.

The clubroom had suffered as great a change as I had, but in the opposite direction. From being a bright and friendly room it had turned into an open-plan office. A large blow-up of the Ordnance Survey map was spread on the deep bar-top and was being covered with symbols denoting, I supposed, the positions in which every cigarette-end or dog-plonk had been found. Screens and chalkboards from some unexplained source obscured the pastel walls and displayed lists and diagrams.

The plastic-topped tables had been assembled into two clumps. At one, uniformed and plain-clothes juniors, male and female, were sifting papers, compiling more lists and charts and either competing for the single telephone or using radios. At the other, on which had been laid out some shotguns and several cartridge cartons now containing polythene bags which I presumed held whatever was considered to be potential evidence, Superintendent McHarg sat with a man in uniform who, from the style of his uniform and the amount of silver on it, I assumed to be a very senior cookie indeed, outranking even Chief Superintendent Munro.

Seven or eight men in plain clothes sat facing these two, but back from the tables to indicate subordinate status. The police, it seemed, had as subtle a pecking order as a Women's Institute.

As we approached what I thought of as the 'top table',

Superintendent McHarg got to his feet. This little courtesy started a chain reaction as first one man and then another stood up. It spread to the serfs, who rose hesitantly as if surprised to find that it could happen. Soon, only the WPCs were sitting.

The Sergeant placed a chair for me at the end of the 'top table' – another subtle differentiation, showing that I was not a member of either party but something strange and separate. I sat down and the men subsided.

'Miss Calder is a gunsmith,' the Superintendent said without any very great conviction. 'I understand that she also shoots at clay pigeons.' His tone and words suggested that it was unlikely that I ever hit any of them.

Allies can appear in the most unexpected places. 'Miss Calder,' said the man with the silver braid, 'was in the finals of the Women's National Skeet Championship last year and the semifinals of the Open.'

The statement was made flatly but McHarg's mouth pursed for a moment as a tiny whisper of amusement could be heard in the room. 'I didn't know that. Mr Beamington is the Assistant Chief Constable (Crime),' he explained to me.

Mr Beamington nodded seriously but when he met my eye I detected some deep amusement. His uniform cap made him less of an individual than a symbolic figure, but when I tried to picture him without it my memory threw up first a tweed cap and then dark hair streaked with distinguished silver at the temple. The penny dropped. I had encountered him as a guest on several shoots which I had attended as a humble beater. I was about to return his testimonial by mentioning, truthfully, that he was a first-class game shot, but he gave me a tiny headshake and I held my peace. In view of the fanatical anti-gun views held by some of the head men in both police and government, an ambitious officer might well be reticent about that particular hobby.

Mr McHarg decided against any further introductions

and got down to business. He led me quickly through the reasons why Mr Tullos could not have died accidentally, or at least not in the place and manner which somebody had tried to suggest, and through what I inferred from the unbroken clays and fired cartridges which I had pointed out to the Sergeant. I had had a minor role in several of Dad's court cases, so I was able to make a clear and succinct statement. When I had finished, he nodded.

One of the men raised a hand, but the Superintendent frowned at him. 'Questions later. Miss Calder, can you help us to identify any of these guns? If so, don't touch them, point them out.'

'For starters,' I said, 'I believe that the two muzzle-loaders belonged to the dead man.' I pointed to a reproduction percussion shotgun by Pedersoli and a beautiful double flintlock by Rhoades. 'He was a black-powder enthusiast and I've seen him practising with them. The modern gun which was found beside him looks very like the one he always used, and since there's nothing similar here it seems a safe assumption that it was his.

'The Beretta S Oh Three—' I pointed it out in case some ignoramus failed to recognise the unusual side-plates and action-body '—was definitely a club gun. I replaced a broken striker in it only a month ago. The Winchester and the Mario Beschi look very like club guns which I've seen in general use for years – the Winchester was gifted to the club by a member who was going abroad and the other, I think, was a bequest. The Krieghoff I haven't seen before; but it's a twenty-bore, so if it's a club gun it wouldn't have seen much use. That only leaves the Browning. It may be a club gun or it may belong to a member who's left it here for safe-keeping.'

'Thank you,' Mr McHarg said. 'Questions?'

The man who had raised his hand repeated the gesture. 'One thing sticks in my craw,' he said. 'Putting the body beside a trap-house where the accident could not have happened seems such an elementary mistake. Does

57

it suggest somebody who was unfamiliar with clay pigeon shooting?'

'That's hardly a question for Miss Calder,' Superintendent McHarg said. 'If there's nothing else. . . ?'

'I would like to answer the question,' I said carefully. There was a sudden stillness in the room. 'I did think that at first. I have since had time to go for a walk outside the club fencing while I waited. I noticed that the embankment between the club and the neighbouring development – the timeshare and the Country Club and so on – is flat-topped. It would make an attractive place for a picnic when no shooting was going on. There's a sort of barbecue pit with fluffy wood-ash in it. Yesterday was windy until late afternoon so that, although there's some screening by whin-bushes, the ash would have blown around if it had been there longer than last night. If somebody was up on the mound, they could see every trap-house at the lower level. But the Skeet trap-houses are screened by the safety walls. Of course, he might still have had to move the body there. . .'

Assistant Chief Constable (Crime) Beamington was grinning all over his face.

'Thank you, Miss Calder,' Mr McHarg said with finality.

Sergeant Fellowes touched my shoulder. 'I'll run you home,' he said.

This time, nobody stood up.

FIVE

Sergeant Fellowes, who had previously treated me as if I were a favourite but tomboyish younger sister, held the car door for me and closed it gently. The car, I guessed, was his own. It was a Vauxhall of dull colour, neither large nor new but clean and tidy and kept with a more personal care than the police would have given to a pool car, and the accumulation of odds and ends – sunglasses, tissues and scribbling materials predominating – seemed more like one man's impedimenta. It was a car like a million others on the road – a car from which observation could be kept without attracting any attention.

The Sergeant seemed amused. 'That was a bit of a facer you gave the Super, about our murderer's options being limited by an observer up on the embankment,' he said. He drove well, I noticed.

'It wasn't meant to be,' I said.

'I know that. You have the sort of well-meaning innocence that catches other people flat-footed and red-faced. I rather think that Mr McHarg was waiting to spring it himself, in his best "Who would look after you idiots if I wasn't there to blow your noses and wipe your bottoms?" manner.'

If I did not recognise myself in his evaluation, at least the thoughts which he attributed to Superintendent McHarg accorded with my own impression of his superior. I gathered that Sergeant Fellowes liked him as little as I did.

'I was only trying to be helpful. Did I steal his thunder?'

'You did. And in front of the ACC. He'll mention you in his prayers tonight.'

'Maybe I need a prayer or two.'

He chuckled. 'And maybe I'll say one for you as I kneel beside my lonely bed tonight.' I thought that he placed a tiny stress on the word 'lonely', as if he dared to think that I might even be wondering whether he was married or cohabiting.

Privately, I decided that the Superintendent was not the sort of person whose prayers would receive immediate attention. 'It served him right for being such a grouch,' I said. 'And for having such a big audience. Does a murder always take such a big team?'

'When there isn't an obvious suspect. Ninety-nine per cent of all that information will turn out to be irrelevant but the other one per cent will be essential. If we knew which one per cent, we could save a lot of manpower.'

'If I've got to run the place from midday Thursday,' I said, 'can I have the club's guns back?'

'I don't see why not. It's not as if gunshots figured in the case. Once they've been examined for prints and when cartridges have been fired out of them for comparison, we won't need them any more. I'll see if I can get them back to you by Thursday afternoon. Of course, if one of them fired the cartridges in that bin we'll need to hold on to it.'

'Just so long as I have guns for visitors to borrow,' I said.

He took his eyes of the road for a second. 'Should you be lending firearms to visitors?'

'The club has an Exemption Certificate,' I said. 'And a shotgun isn't a firearm under the Act. Surely it's better that one of the timeshare visitors uses a club gun instead of bringing his own gun on holiday to where there isn't any provision for security?' I waited to see whether he would ask any more questions. Some police officers know less about the 1968 Firearms Act than the average shooter.

His mind was on another tack. 'You needn't worry about being alone up there,' he said.

'I wasn't going to.'

'Oh? I thought that the idea of being on your own at the scene of a murder, with the murderer still on the loose, might have made you nervous.'

If that was my cue to be fluttery and dependent, I let it go by. 'It didn't until you started going on about it,' I said.

'Well, it needn't. There will have to be an officer with you, waiting to identify anybody who turns up, take statements and collect fired cartridges.'

I sighed, loudly in order to be heard over the hum of the car. 'Pretending to be a regular but holding the gun upside down?'

'Very probably. How well did you know Mr Tullos?'

I shrugged, for all the good that that would do. The Sergeant, like the good driver that he was, was studying the road ahead. 'He was just a face,' I said. 'The face which sold everything from cartridges to snacks, took entries and arranged competitions. The face I told to go and boil its head when it tried to get me to keep my dog on a lead.'

'All the same, if you shot there even once a month you must have been in his company, if only as part of the same crowd, for a total of some hours. What were your impressions of him?'

I thought back to the living, breathing Herbert Tullos, who seemed to be fading from memory already. I wondered whether I was remembering him or the description of him which I had given to the Superintendent. 'Middle-aged, going on elderly,' I said. 'Sandy – he had managed to go almost bald without going grey first, unless he was touching up the pathetic remnant. Slightly rat-faced without looking nasty, if you can imagine it – but you've seen him, of course.'

'He wasn't looking his best.'

'I suppose not. He was a good shot in spite of his disability. But, when you come to think of it, shooting's one of the few sports at which a man with a damaged leg can compete on equal terms with others.'

'But his character?'

'Surly,' I said. 'Most of the time, he was a grumbler, the sort who puts your back up. And yet, when he let himself go, he could be entertaining. Telling stories.'

'Do you remember any of them?'

'Not really. Mostly, they were stories from his police days, Crooks I Have Known. The only one that comes back to me . . . '

'Yes?'

'. . . was the most recent, because it's fresh in my mind. It was last Sunday. I only went along because I was getting out of practice. There's a FITASC Grand Prix coming along next month and I want to compete. Then the season will be on us soon and my Dad won't let me forget it if I let him down. We were having a fifty-bird Sporting shoot. There were about twenty men in it and me, but I'd have won it if I hadn't gone to pieces on the last stand. Anyway, the trap in the tower had been going all weekend. The magazine ran out and clays had to be fetched from the clubhouse. While somebody went for them – Mr Tullos was always excused that duty if possible, because of his leg – he told the story of his last days in the police. Do you know about that?'

'His police career and its abrupt end is almost the sum total of what we've found out about him, thanks to yourself, so far, but let's have his version.'

'The way he told it, he got a call over the radio that an intruder had been seen on the flat roof of a jeweller's shop. He got up there just as a man came up out of a skylight carrying a plastic carrier-bag and a sawn-off shotgun. There was what he called "a bit of an argie-bargie", and the upshot was that he took a load of shot in the leg. By that time, there were police around the building. The man tried to take a jump to the next roof and fell into the alley.

'Mr Tullos – Sergeant Tullos he was then, I think – was carted off to hospital with a badly shattered knee. And who should turn up in the same ward but the man who'd shot him. Several beds away, he said, or there might have been more bloodshed. Why would a criminal be taken to an ordinary hospital?' I asked.

'At that moment he hadn't been convicted of anything, so technically he wasn't a criminal. A prisoner on remand in custody might be treated in a prison hospital, but not if his condition was serious.'

'I see. Later, some of Mr Tullos's police colleagues brought him up a huge basket of fruit. So he hobbled round the ward with it, complete with crutch and a plaster cast. By that time, he was beginning to feel a bit sorry for the man, who was having a bad time with some spinal damage. He hadn't told the others in the ward who the man was, so he felt that he couldn't leave him out. And then, he said, the bastard – that's what he called him – went and took a large bunch of grapes, the only grapes in the basket. The other patients had been too polite to be so greedy and Mr Tullos had been looking forward to having them himself. He said that that annoyed him more than being shot, because it made it more personal.

'Mr Tullos's knee never recovered and he was retired from the police with a pension and a few thousand under the Criminal Injuries Compensation Act – which, he said, he blew within a few months. That's all there was to it, but he made quite a funny story out of it. He was probably spinning a yarn.'

'He wasn't,' said Sergeant Fellowes. 'He was playing it down, but that's broadly what happened. He left something out. He was awarded the Queen's Police Medal. The man Cairns – he was known as "Joukie" – had been a partner in a whole series of bigger robberies, some of them with violence. He was a very tough character and Sergeant Tullos knew it. Some of his colleagues felt that Tullos qualified for the Queen's Medal for Being a Bloody Idiot, but the highheidyins often prefer not to see it that way.'

We were nearly home. I thought that I had never known Mr Tullos. The middle-aged cripple must once have been a young man with fire in his belly. 'I wish I'd known that,' I said sadly. 'He gave the impression that the whole thing was one big accident. He said that the other thing that really made him angry was that Cairns would only have got a few hundred for his haul when he fenced it, if he'd got away, but he'd sawn off a stolen shotgun by W. and C. Scott which would have fetched ten times as much.'

'And you sympathised with that viewpoint?' the Sergeant asked.

'Of course,' I said. 'To me, that was equivalent to wiping his backside on the Mona Lisa. If you knew the work and artistry that goes into a Best English handmade gun. . .'

'I'll take your word for it,' he said. I could tell that he was trying to hide amusement. 'Do you know anything else about Mr Tullos? There are still many gaps in his biography. Sometimes these little anecdotes help to plug a hole.'

Another picture came to my mind, of Herbert Tullos, in perky mood, with his blue club cap pushed to the back of his head, leaning across the clubroom bar and keeping a group of members in stitches while the rain which had ended shooting for the moment bounced off the cars outside. 'Sir Peter said that he spent most of the years between in a desk job for an oil company, but he must have been in Africa at one time. Zimbabwe, I think he said.'

Following my directions, the Sergeant had brought us to the door of Briesland House, but he made no move to get out. It was warm and quiet in the car. The Sergeant smelled of fresh, male sweat, not displeasing. The garden was bright with flowers and the old house glowed in the sunshine. Sergeant Fellowes let his eyes rest on the stonework. I never usually noticed the house – it was where I had always lived. But now, seeing it through his eyes, I realised that it looked opulent, as if it never expected anybody to worry about money within its walls. If so, we must often have been a disappointment to it. Dad had bought the house with an insurance company reward before I was born and the place was his great pride.

'We knew about the oil company,' he said, frowning, 'but there's a year missing. What was he doing in Zimbabwe?'

'That I can't tell you. I know he made some money there because he still had it but couldn't get it out. That was one of his tales. Another from that time. . .'

'Go on,' he said. 'Anything might help us to track him through that missing year.'

'This won't,' I told him. 'But it may help you to understand him, as he was after he was crippled. His stories usually had a cruel twist in them somewhere.

'He said that he managed to keep up with his shooting. There was a lot of good sport to be had out there, but he was very dependent on a pair of pointers.'

'Dogs, you mean?'

The Sergeant, I was reminded, knew very little about shooting. 'Dogs which seek out the game and then wait "on point" for you to come up. And then they flush the quarry. He said that his dogs were very good up to that moment, but once the quarry was up they broke discipline and chased it out of sight. A dangerous habit,' I explained, 'and not calculated to fill the bag.

'Slowed down by his leg, he found all the usual re-training methods beyond him, so he resorted to the electric collar. That's a gadget that you put round a dog's neck and when you need to inflict punishment at a distance you press a button on a radio controller and the dog gets a painful electric shock. It's frowned on by most trainers, but it does get results in some cases.

'When he tried it out, the bitch yelped and came back to heel. In a fortnight, she was completely cured of chasing. But when the male chased after a guinea-fowl he paid no attention to the electric collar. Mr Tullos could hardly believe that the dog was so wrapped up in the chase that the pain meant nothing to him, so he sat down in the shadow of a tall hedge and took the collar to bits. The circuitry seemed all right and there was still power in the batteries.

'The native bearer who was with him seemed very much intrigued by all this technology. So Mr Tullos explained that this was "white man's magic" and buckled the collar round the bearer's neck. The bearer was as pleased as Punch and strutted off round the end of the hedge.

'Mr Tullos pressed the button.'

The Sergeant gave a snort of amusement.

'It isn't the sort of story you should laugh at, in this day and age,' I said severely. 'But he told it well. His description of the bearer, eyes popping and hair suddenly straightened out, coming back over the hedge with about three feet to spare, had his audience falling about. He told it in the bar when we were rained off, about a year ago. And when the rain stopped and the competition re-started, I don't think that anybody hit anything. Every time somebody called for a bird, somebody else would snicker and he'd crack up again.'

The Sergeant sat in silence for a full minute. He managed to control his laughter but I saw him wipe his eyes when he spoke again his voice was not quite steady.

'You didn't tell us that you'd been at the club on Sunday,' he said.

'Nobody asked me.'

'Who else was present?'

'When I think back,' I said, 'I see a whole lot of faces but I'm not sure which day I'm remembering. Mr Tullos always filed the score-cards, because we have handicap competitions sometimes. They're in a big blue box-file. I've seen him bring it out when somebody quibbled about the handicap he'd been given. You'd find that a more reliable source than my memory. Why are you interested in Sunday?'

'Who knows when it all began?' he said. 'Tell me, what were you doing on Monday evening?'

'I was here, with my uncle.' I tried not to sound hurt. From his viewpoint, I could have killed Mr Tullos as easily as anybody could. And if I had not, the sooner the police could clear me of suspicion the better.

'And what are you doing next Sunday evening? I gather that you'll be off duty. And so will I.'

His effrontery took my breath away. He was a racist and apparently I was a suspect and here he was trying to make a date with me. 'Would you have asked that question if you'd known that my father was only the butler here?' I asked him.

My question struck home, but not in the way that I had intended. He leaned back and shouted with laughter. 'Definitely,' he said when his voice came back. 'Even if I didn't know who your father was.'

'Well,' I said, 'on Sunday evening I'm de-frosting the fridge.'

I got out of the car, not waiting for the door to be opened for me and quite forgetting about Sam. 'Our first quarrel,' he said. 'Can I keep the dog?'

'No, you can't,' I said, turning back.

He was still laughing as he drove away. I could not think whether to laugh, swear or kick poor old Sam.

When I entered, neutralising the alarm system from the hall cupboard, the house felt dead. There was no smell of cooking and no sign of Uncle Ronnie. In my irritation with the Sergeant I was about to call down curses upon Ronnie's grizzled head when I found a note from him on the kitchen table, saying that we were bidden to eat with Janet and Wallace. If the word 'bidden' seems extreme in the context, it is still the right word; Janet's invitations were thinly veiled commands.

Priority Number One was to feed Sam. Number Two was a quick shower and a more suitable selection of clean clothes. Feeling more human, I reset the alarms and the timer which switches lights and a radio on and off and sent Sam to his bed. If Dad had not been a gunsmith, he could have been a wow as a professional dog-trainer. Sam had been taught to stay in his bed until he heard a stranger in the house, after which he was free to come through the dog-door from the back porch, thereby setting off the alarms, and to take whatever action he deemed necessary. Sam was one of the mildest of Labradors, but if the family territory was threatened he could be a tiger. And, like all Labradors, he always believed himself to be near starvation. It has never happened yet, but I always expect to come home and find a burglar reduced to mincemeat and a pair of shoes.

The family car was in a security compound near Liverpool and Ronnie had his Land-rover away with him, but I had keys to Dad's jeep and permission to use it very carefully if at all. On the long and slightly downhill straight into Newton Lauder, with the low sun blazing between the roadside trees in a quick, lighthouse rhythm, I wound the jeep up to a noisy gallop but, as usual, it refused to touch the ton. Some day with a following wind. . .

In the Square, I parked where the shadow of the buildings would soon fall across the jeep – I hate getting into a car with hot seats. The shop was closed up tight for the night. It is not small as shops go, although its old-fashioned style and proportions make it seem poky in comparison to the supermarket next door. Dad and Wal, who have seen the business grow from the time when the shop was an echoing emptiness, never seem to notice the clutter; but they have managed to cram a disproportionate amount of stock into its limited space. Janet complains eternally.

To me, the shop, with its shelves and racks vanishing high into the tall ceiling, stacked and hung with all the paraphernalia and clothing of fishing and shooting, is a perfect place to visit but hell to serve in. The others know exactly where every knife, trout-fly, oil-bottle or tin of airgun slugs is to be found, but I have to search all the shelves and admit defeat, only to have the item jump into my hand, so to speak, the moment the customer is out of sight. Dad's workshop, and the trading in antique guns, had been squeezed out of the shop and banished to Briesland House around the time I was born.

Beside the shop a panelled door, painted a discreet charcoal grey, let me into a small hall and I climbed a stair to the flat where Mum and Dad had started their life together. I had probably been conceived somewhere in its few rooms. Janet met me on the landing.

When I was young, Janet seemed terribly old, although she is a few years younger than Mum. But while Mum has spread a little over the years and never bothers to hide the grey in her hair, Janet has never changed; as I approached adulthood she even seemed, like Sir Peter, to grow younger by comparison. She still has some of the golden prettiness which must first have attracted Wal, but while she sometimes, quite deliberately, gives the impression of being a dumb blonde she is as sharp as a knife and almost as hard. I don't mean hard in the sense of cruel, but firm and unsentimental. Her one human trait, apart from her affection for Wal, is her curiosity.

She led me into their living-room, where Ronnie and Wallace were already lolling at ease, and gave me a very weak gin and tonic. Janet is one of the few who realise that I have actually grown up, so I gave her the benefit of the doubt and assumed that the dilution of the drink was because of my new status as a driver. The dining-table had been pulled out from under the window and laid for four.

She vanished into the kitchenette for a moment and reappeared with a tall glass of sherry. 'What was all the fuss and flapdoodle about?' she asked me from the door. 'The police were looking for you during the morning and Sir Peter phoned later to ask whether your services could be spared. Ronnie knows, but he won't say.'

'It's little enough I know about it,' Ronnie said, 'and Sir Peter said to hold my wheesht.'

'A small consultancy job for the police,' I said airily, just to see the look on their faces.

Janet's face was disappointingly dubious. 'You mean you're a witness?'

'No. They just wanted an expert opinion about something. It'll be in tomorrow's papers, so it can't hurt to tell you about it.'

She glanced back into the kitchenette and registered frustration. 'I'm going to serve the soup,' she said suddenly. 'Move to the table. And don't you dare to say another word, Deborah, until I come back.'

'It would b-break her heart to miss a word,' Wal said. ''Specially if there's a scandal brewing.' Wallace is lean, with a bony and rather clever face; which is only fair because he's a rather clever man. He is also a nice, mild man (only Dad can ever make him lose his temper) with a gentle sense of humour. He has a reputation as a financial wizard, but his career in accountancy was cut short by the loss of three fingers from his right hand in an accident, despite which he is a surprisingly good shot. He has a slight, natural stammer which usually disappears as he settles down.

'No scandal,' I said. 'Mystery, but so far a disappointing lack of scandal.'

He moved to the table. I suddenly felt ravenous after my long and under-nourished day. I was even hungry enough to fancy soup despite the hot weather, but Janet served it scalding hot – on purpose, I suspect. I nibbled on delicious, crusty bread with butter and while I waited for the soup to cool I told them about the death of Herbert Tullos and my own invaluable contribution to the investigation. Looking back, I may have given the impression that the police had begged me to come and take a leading role in an investigation which would otherwise get nowhere. If so, blame the occasions when I had been overshadowed by Dad and patronised by the others.

'Are they going to p-pay you for your work?' Wal wanted to know. I said that I hadn't the faintest idea and he cast his eyes up to the ceiling. Wallace does not really care about money for its own sake. To him, money represents the counters in a huge game which he plays against the rest of the world in general and HM Inspector of Taxes in particular; a game which he plays to win with the abstract dedication of a snakes and ladders enthusiast.

My uncle wanted to know the gorier details, Wallace was interested in the technicalities while Janet was more curious about the Sergeant. Either my voice had betrayed a certain interest or Sir Peter had been gossiping again. Before we got round to Sir Peter's request for my services, soup was finished and the meat course was on the table. The lamb was perfection but the potatoes, I noticed, were slightly hard in the middle. Janet's curiosity had driven her to hurry the meal onto the table.

Sir Peter, I discovered, had been busy. He did not want the clubhouse empty and the whole layout open to vandalism. He could probably have persuaded me to stay in the living quarters of the clubhouse overnight, even alone, but he had decided that that would be an unsuitable job for a girl. So Ronnie was to spend his nights in the clubhouse. And because I must not be alone in Briesland House (whether for fear of intruders or for reasons of chaperonage was never made clear) Janet would move in with me.

'That's a bit hard on Uncle Wal, isn't it?' I suggested.

'Glad of the p-peace and quiet,' Wal said.

Janet was in the middle of enquiring whether the Sergeant was married. She is eternally on the hunt for a husband suitable for me – according to her standard of suitability rather than his sex appeal or my taste in men. It took a few seconds for Wal's words to sink in.

'And just what does that mean?' she asked.

It probably had not meant anything, but the prospect of freedom from Janet's powerful presence had gone to Wallace's head. 'It's the snoring,' he said. 'Deborah, if you're being paid to keep the clay club running—'

'A pittance,' I said.

'—you'll be doing it in the firm's time.'

'Mostly evenings and weekends,' I pointed out.

'I do not snore,' Janet said. 'And you told Deborah that we didn't need her in the shop, so it's none of your business if she earns a little pin-money.'

'Unless we both have to go out,' Wal reminded her. 'In which case, we'll have to pay Minnie to take over. Perhaps it isn't the snoring as much as the little popping sound in between.'

'I'll buy any clays and cartridges through the shop,' I promised. 'I'm to keep the club's profit on cartridges, so if you make me turn in my pittance I'll buy them where I can get them cheapest.'

Wal thought it over and then nodded. He had made his opening gambit and I had replied with the appropriate move. Honour was satisfied.

'I definitely do not snore,' Janet said with finality. She is always the last to see that her leg is being pulled. 'Who'd want to knock off Mr Tullos? Deborah, you and your father were up there on Sunday. Who was there?'

'Just faces. You know how it is. The scorer calls for Charlie and the face which discussed pigeon shooting with you the week before steps forward. Sir Peter gave the Sergeant a run-down of the members and the most regular visitors and I identified most of them in my mind, but they've faded again. There were a few strangers there, but Dad would have known the rest.'

'Were there any of the usual arguments?' Wal asked.

'Everyone seemed a little friendlier than usual. There were no disputes over the scoring and hardly any back-biting. Mr Tullos seemed to be in one of his better moods.'

'That probably accounted for the general sweetness and light,' Janet said. 'He could be a devil when he felt like it. His limp probably gave him a grudge against the world.'

'All the same,' I said unhappily, 'it needn't have been someone from the club who killed him. He could have made all sorts of enemies.' I was already developing a motherly feeling towards the club and all its regulars.

'I doubt that,' said Ronnie. 'Sir Peter used to send me up to give him a hand, when something heavy needed shifting. He was aye there. It was as if he'd no other life at a' – except when he was away at the shoots.'

'I've always wondered,' Janet said, 'how an ex-policeman managed to afford quite so many trips to the big competitions. He always stayed at a good hotel. I' n sure he never won enough to cover his expenses.'

'He had at least two pensions,' Wal pointed out, 'plus his salary and perks at the club. And he wasn't always too scrupulous.'

'He wasn't ripping off the club, was he?' I asked him anxiously. If there was any shortage of cash or assets I would want it identified before I took over.

'I think not. But he often needled one or other of the better-heeled shooters into a private challenge match for sums which weren't exactly chicken-feed. He threw out a challenge to me once and when I turned him down he made some sneering remark about being afraid even to shoot against another cripple.' Wallace glanced down for a moment at the stumps of his missing fingers. 'But if I'd taken him up on it, I'd have insisted on inspecting the clays and on opening up a few samples of his cartridges.'

'Looking for what?' I asked. You never know when such tidbits of information may come in useful.

Wallace looked at me with one eyebrow up and then shrugged. 'Flattened small-shot, to give himself a wider spread at Skeet. Clays which had lain in the sun. They sag in the middle, you know, so that they fly at the most peculiar angles. He used to set them aside, saying that it wouldn't do to sell them to one of the other clubs, but there was usually a little stack of them in a corner of each trap-house.'

'The . . . the nasty old gentleman,' I said. If I had uttered the first words which came to my mind, Janet would certainly have repeated them to Mum. I had once been fool enough to accept a challenge from Mr Tullos to a match at Skeet and somehow I had found that I was backing myself far more heavily than I had expected. It had seemed to me that he had shot above his usual form and I had certainly shot below mine. 'That could have given some of the regular attenders a motive for getting cross with him. People have been murdered for less.' I had no intention of admitting that that little episode had occurred, let alone that it had cost me fifty quid, the loss of which had been very difficult to conceal.

'Very much less,' Wallace agreed. 'And then there was the question of the proposed takeover.'

'Are you suggesting that somebody from the Leisure Complex knocked him off?' I asked. 'According to Sir Peter, he was dead against the takeover.'

'But was he?' Wal retorted. 'Your much loved godfather may not have been frank with you – or with the police. About a fortnight ago, one of the timeshare guests phoned me, wanting to know if we had a carbon-fibre trout rod in stock. He bought one over the phone. I was curious to see the Country Club, so I took the rod up to him and we had a drink together. Herb Tullos was coming out of the manager's office, looking like the cat that stole the cream. I think that he'd been got at.'

'And he was on the committee,' I said.

'The committee couldn't have taken a decision to sell up. I warned Sir Peter that if the subject came up at an Extraordinary General Meeting I thought that Tullos might have changed his tune.'

'For money?'

'That or the promise of the managership.'

'Managership of what?' I demanded. 'I thought they wanted to close the place down.'

'A potential money-spinner like that? They want to

take it over and turn it into a commercial operation. Sponsored competitions, television coverage and all that jazz. They already do good winter business out of the English and Italians who come for the grouse. A really top-flight clay pigeon set-up within their control would round out their operation very nicely, thank you. One of the Country Club members leaked it to me. He has a foot in both camps. He brought in a Miroku Seven Thousand, by the way. He wants a fatter recoil pad fitted. And it's in a hurry because his two weeks in the timeshare runs out on Saturday.'

I pulled a face. I had been counting on one more day of leisure before my new duties began.

'If I snore,' Janet said, 'you've taken a hell of a long time to complain about it.'

Wallace nodded. 'I'm like that,' he said comfortably.

SIX

My day of leisure went completely down the plug-hole. I spent some of the Wednesday on the Miroku which Wal had taken in. Wallace collected it at lunchtime, leaving in its place a side-by-side game gun which had been brought in for a general overhaul. (This usually meant that the innards would be a mass of rust, which the owner would refuse to believe when confronted by a bill for the man-hours entailed.) I would have got on with it straight away, but the afternoon went to pot when Sir Peter called in to brief me on what I could and could not do at the Gun Club.

I fed Ronnie and we spent the evening in the garden. Dad would hit the ceiling if he came home to find that his beloved garden had gone back to the Indians. And quite right, too, I admitted to myself. We helped the tedious time to pass by composing rude limericks. Ronnie's were ruder, but mine rhymed and scanned better.

I slept lightly, haunted by dreams of disaster. I was going to make a fool of myself. Or they would sell the club. Or the murderer would return.

Thursday came in at last, still bright, still hot. The farmers, who could have found fault with the weather even if they had chosen it themselves, would soon be prophesying doom and famine. I dressed with care. I did not want to be hot, but I was damned if I was going to be as Plain Jane as I had been two days earlier; nor had I any intention of ruining my few good clothes. I settled for last year's best cotton and fairly sensible shoes.

I was not due to open up the Pentland Gun Club until after lunch, but I wanted to spend some time, before the arrival of any possible visitors, familiarising myself with what was where and why. So I put Sam and my twenty-bore into the back of the jeep. As an afterthought, I added the game gun which had come in for a service.

Traffic was heavy on the main road and I had to crawl behind an articulated jumbo for miles. After that I was onto the tight and twisty country roads and climbing steadily. I came up past the dam without ever having been over forty. It was boring, but it was not the boredom which worried me. I always feel safer at speed because there is less temptation for my butterfly mind to wander.

The gates of the Pentland Gun Club were closed and locked. No cars were to be seen other than Mr Tullos's van. There was no sign of the promised police presence. This I found disconcerting. I had duplicate keys from Sir Peter. I drove inside and took a quick look round, but there was no constable lying dead or unconscious among the stands and trap-house.

The police seemed to have left the place reasonably tidy. I let myself into the clubroom, gave it a sweep and then studied the notice-board. Mr Tullos seemed to have brought it up to date before meeting his end. There was a charity shoot with large prizes to be held near Glasgow on Saturday and a qualifying shoot for the National DTL Championship at Cumbernauld, so it would be a comparatively quiet weekend back at the club. As usual, the charity shoot would accept ladies for a slightly reduced entrance fee but would preclude them from the major prizes. One of the last surviving bastions of sex discrimination. I decided to write to my MP, whoever he was.

With a jump, I realised that somebody was watching me from the doorway. He was a stocky man, slightly overweight, with thinning, sandy hair and a disgruntled expression spread like rancid butter over an already peevish face. He was carefully dressed and groomed, but the effect

77

was spoiled by the sweat which trickled down his face and stained his lightweight suit under the arms.

'Just who might you be?' he asked. His tone suggested that he might neither believe nor approve of whatever answer I made, so I decided to side-step.

'Are you a member?' I asked. I tried to insinuate that even if he wasn't black-balled he couldn't afford to join.

'No, I am not. I'm the manager of the Leisure Complex. McGruer's the name.' His tone shifted from angry to plaintive. 'Look, what the hell's going on around here?'

'I'm Deborah Calder. I'm standing in for the steward and I don't know any more than was in yesterday's papers,' I said – not quite truthfully, because the death had been covered by about three lines in most papers and a dozen words at the end of the television news, and the wording had suggested that while the death had been an accident the police were looking into it, just to determine whether there had been negligence. The press release by the police must have been evasive to the point of being deliberately misleading.

He came further into the room. 'You are, are you?' He paused and blinked pale eyelids at me. 'Will you have a seat on the committee?'

His sudden interest was so blatant that I almost laughed at him. 'I shouldn't think so. Anyway, selling out wouldn't be a matter for the committee. It would go to a Special General Meeting. And I'd be against selling.'

'There could be a lot of money to share out. And it isn't as if we'd close the place down. It's just that we'd like all the facilities under the one management, so that we can control the times of noise-making and prevent clashes of dates.'

'Balls,' I said. 'Aren't you going to offer me the managership?'

He was silent for some seconds. He was a very transparent man and I could see his little mind ticking over, finding my name in a card-index and working out that I knew more than he would have liked but that I was only the daughter of a member and that Dad was already opposed to a sell-out. 'There's more to it than was in the papers,' he said suddenly, 'or why are the police coming round, over and over again, harassing our residents? Who's been putting in the poison?'

'I wouldn't know,' I said. 'Don't ask me, ask the police. Anyway, why are you getting so uptight about it?'

His face darkened again and he took a step towards me. 'Don't be pert,' he said. 'You can do without making enemies around here. A girl on her own—'

'But it was a good question,' said Sergeant Fellowes. He followed Mr McGruer in through the open door. I hoped that the quick look he gave me contained a trace of unpolicemanlike warmth. 'Good morning again, Mr McGruer. Why don't you want us speaking to your residents?'

Mr McGruer flushed red. 'When the residents get upset, who do you think they complain to?'

The Sergeant shrugged. 'I can't see why they would complain to you, when there's a perfectly satisfactory official Complaints Procedure. It's not as though you could do a damn thing about it – except by helping us to clear up the mess quickly instead of obstructing us.'

'I don't know what you mean,' Mr McGruer said.

'You know exactly what I mean. I've just come back from the timeshare flats. You knew that we wanted to speak to whichever residents were out and about on Monday evening late. You knew that we were having difficulty catching some of them at home.'

'They come here on holiday,' Mr McGruer protested, 'not to sit indoors in this sort of weather. Some of them go touring and stay away for a night or two.'

'You begged us, on bended knee, not to make any more door-to-door enquiries. You promised me that you would find out for me who had been out late that evening. Your manner, Mr McGruer, was not convincing. I have just come back from knocking on a few doors. You have spoken to absolutely nobody on the subject. Why not? Mr McGruer, what are you trying to hide?'

Mr McGruer tried to bluff and he tried to bluster but the Sergeant was not to be put off. In the end, McGruer could only fall back on the argument that his guests were entitled to their privacy.

'If by that you mean what I think you mean,' the Sergeant said grimly, 'I may as well tell you that we are not the least bit interested in the morals of your timeshare residents. If any of them were committing fornication, adultery, sodomy or even bestiality up on that embankment on Monday night, I am only interested in what they saw over the fence. But that I mean to have by hook or by crook.

'This is Thursday. On Saturday, some of your timeshare residents will be handing over their units and scattering. I can't wait that long. So if whoever was up there on Monday evening doesn't contact me here by five p.m. tonight, your development will be flooded with officers tomorrow. And it won't bother me one damn bit if your residents are queueing right round the golf course for a turn at crying on your shoulder.'

'If there was anybody,' Mr McGruer said miserably, 'they may not have seen anything. They may have been up there at the wrong time.'

'Or they may have had eyes only for each other. If that's the case, I want to know it. I want to see anybody who was up there between noon and midnight. And if anybody was out for an evening sail at this end of the reservoir, I want to meet them too. You haven't got long so you'd better get going.' He looked at me again and this time I was sure that we were still exchanging little signals. I warmed still more to a man who could let my peevishness of the Tuesday evening pass over his head. 'I left my car at the Country Club. Would you lift me along to collect it? Perhaps we'd have room for Mr McGruer as well? He seems to have walked.'

'There's only a dog-bed in the back of the jeep,' I said, 'and there's one dog in it already.'

Mr McGruer walked. We overtook him outside the gates, stamping furiously along the roadside and slashing at the taller weeds with his stick. When he heard us coming, he made an effort to seem unconcerned.

'As you'll have gathered,' Sergeant Fellowes said, 'I drew the double duty of keeping observation here and seeing that no villain jumps on you. I volunteered for it.'

I would have liked to see his face, but we were approaching a blind hump and I dared not take my eyes off the road. 'I'm flattered,' I said.

'Don't be too flattered. It was that, or becoming swallowed up in endless – and usually profitless – inquiries into the backgrounds and movements of the members and of such recent visitors as we've so far been able to trace.'

'But why were you lurking out of sight?' I asked him.

'I might have learned something.'

'And did you?'

'I've confirmed that you're very innocent and that our Mr McGruer isn't to be trusted. And I knew both of those already.'

Whether that was a compliment or not depended on which shade of meaning you attached to the word 'innocent'. 'You seem to be trusting him rather a lot,' I said.

He laughed shortly. 'We'd already been round such residents as were at home in the units, to ask whose cars travelled this road on Monday evening. When we started to go round again in search of anybody who took a stroll in the direction of the embankment, that's when they started to complain and Mr McGruer did his proverbial nut. Putting together the gossip we've picked up so far, the answers to the who-was-where and doing-what-to-whom enquiry and the questions people refused to answer, we're pretty sure we know who was up there for a picnic and a cuddle on Monday night. He's elsewhere just now, visiting, but he'll be back today. What you just heard was more a test of his honesty, and Mr McGruer's.'

'Just him?' I said. 'Not her?'

'She's usually in the company of her husband. We're not in the business of wrecking marriages. We'll choose our moment.'

I let that go by. 'Did anybody see a car?' I asked. 'Or any dinghies sailing down that way?'

'Several people, several cars. One car turned out to belong to the farmer. I'm told that it was a bit too breezy for the inland mariners.'

'The wind dropped later . . . at home,' I said. 'It may still have been blowing here.'

We turned off what could loosely be described as the main road onto a driveway. Sam woke up and snuffled in my ear. He knew that there were guns in the car.

For the first time I could see the golf course and the Country Club. Golfers were out and riders were mounting. Dinghies were jilling around in the light airs. Around the timeshare units some plushy cars, and several of quite remarkable scruffiness, were parked. (The truly rich do not need status symbols.) The landscaping still had to mature, but already the buildings gave an impression of relaxed jollity.

I dropped the Sergeant at his own car and followed him back to the Gun Club. He shook a warning finger as we passed Mr McGruer and I shook two. I parked facing east, so that the sun would be off the seats by the time I was ready to leave. He pulled up beside me. The sun was warm, prickling the skin and heating up the head. I put on my lucky cap – a red, baseball-type cap emblazoned 'Dallas Gun Club', which my friend Simon had brought back from Texas for me and which I always believed put me one up on those with the club's similar but blue cap.

'I have the club's guns in my boot,' the Sergeant said. 'The cartridges in the bin were fired in the dead man's own gun. And it was his own gun, by the way. Sensibly,

he'd kept a record of its serial number in his desk. What
are you going to do now?'

'I must take a walk round and see that all's in order,'
I said. 'What are you going to do?'

He leaned back against his car. 'I'm going to follow you
around like Sam,' he said. 'I'm not convinced that we've
learned all there is to learn from this place. You never
know what scraps of information may come in useful. I
want to be shown how it all works. And you may very
well spot something wrong which looked normal to us.
I wonder . . .'

'Yes?'

'Would you shoot a few of the – what did you call
them? – the stands? You might even give me a lesson. I
could never pass for one of the boys, but I might get by
as a pupil under instruction. Visitors may not talk freely if
they're pounced on by a copper as soon as they roll up.'

'Sneaky,' I said. 'All right. Let's take the guns inside
first. You're not telling me very much, are you?'

He looked surprised. 'Aren't I? Professional habit, I
suppose. We never tell the public more than we have to.'

'I'm not the public, I'm a consultant. What time did
he die?'

'The pathologist thinks late evening. About two hours
after he ate a chocolate bar, if we knew when that was.'

'Had his gun been fired?'

'Yes. What else have I been keeping from you?'

I couldn't think of any more questions. We carried the
guns into the office. They had been cleaned, not well but
adequately. The Winchester was the best fit for him. We
stowed the others in the safe and I locked it again. 'You
have one set of keys,' I said.

He held up the ring. 'I'll keep them for the moment,'
he said.

I supposed that he was within his rights. 'Don't leave
them lying around,' I said. 'Now, I'll let you off with your
tuition fee and the cost of your clays, but if you're going

to shoot you can pay for a day-membership and a box of cartridges.'

He paid up without a murmur although he seemed surprised at how little change he got back out of a tenner. Clay pigeon shooting, as I had told Mr Munro, is not a cheap hobby. I wondered how it would look on his expenses sheet. He hung his jacket in the office and I fitted him with somebody's Skeet vest. 'These are cooler,' I said, 'but you still need two layers of clothing to allow for the friction of recoil. And on the club's behalf I'll present you with a complimentary cap.'

'I never wear a cap,' he smiled.

'You do now. Bits of clay pigeon can come down from a height.' I lent him ear-muffs and protective shooting glasses. He was beginning to look highly professional.

I got my twenty-bore and a belt of cartridges out of the jeep. 'First lesson,' I said. 'You carry the gun open, empty and pointing at the ground or the sky at all times except when ready to shoot. Got that?'

'I've got it,' he said humbly. 'Where do we start? The Skeet?'

'Something easier, for a beginner. But first,' I said, 'let's take a look in here.' I stopped at the big bin which stood at a corner of the clubhouse.

'We looked in there. Nothing but cartridges.'

'Did you stir them up?'

'I didn't,' he said, 'and I don't think any of the others did. We just looked inside and saw exactly what you'd expect to see at a clay pigeon club.'

'But which are on top?' I lifted the lid. The bin was half filled with fired cartridges. In the States, where I had once visited as a member of a women's Skeet team, these would have been a precious asset, saved and re-sold to members – so much so that any spent shell which reaches the ground belongs to the club. In Britain, where reloading is less common, shooters could help themselves or the spent shells would go to the tip.

'They look much of a muchness to me,' the Sergeant said.

'For a start,' I told him, 'Harry Noble kept his appointment on Monday. Those yellow ones on top are twenty-bore.'

'But you were here on Sunday,' he said. He looked down at my cartridges. 'You shoot twenty-bore. Don't you?'

'Not always. And I use Winchesters,' I said, 'not Eley. Most of the rest are club cartridges, but I see some Express. The black ones are Fiocci Trap.'

'So?'

'Damned if I know. You said yourself that you never know what scraps of information may come in useful. If you saved the top few layers, you just might be able to match them up with a gun later. Come on.'

I had to wait while he fetched a plastic bag from his car and skimmed off the top layer of cartridges. Then I led him down the steps and turned away from the Leisure Complex towards where the Gun Club territory petered out among a rocky outcrop and small trees. Here, in a convenient depression, the Bolting Rabbit had been set up – a trap which bowled a special clay pigeon along a grassy strip about twenty yards from the stand. As I walked, I was turning over in my mind the traces which clay shooters leave behind. I had missed something. On more mature thought . . . No, it evaded me.

The Sergeant submitted patiently to a lesson in basic gun-mounting. I unlocked the trap-house and switched on both traps. The magazine was full. As Wal had predicted, a neat stack of slightly warped clays was tucked away in the dark corner. I took out the coiled lead, plugged it into the waterproof socket beside the cage and gave the end to Sergeant Fellowes.

'When I call "Pull," press this tit,' I told him.

I stepped over the bar into the cage, which was shaped like an enlarged telephone booth constructed of tubes and wire mesh and with the door removed.

I scattered the first clay. The sight of the wad skipping

over the grass started me thinking again and I missed the next; but then I hit three in a row, unloaded and stepped out of the cage. 'Your turn,' I said, taking the control from him. 'And take your time. You have longer than you think. Swing through from behind and pull as you go past.'

Something seemed to be worrying him. 'You're sure that this is legal?' he asked.

'The club has an Exemption Certificate. I told you.'

He looked at the cage without favour. 'Do I have to go in there?' he asked. 'It looks cramped. There's only the two of us.'

'Club rule,' I told him. 'It prevents an eager shooter swinging too far. You may as well learn to do it right. Now, no more cold feet. You won't dent the gun.' The tubes around the open side were encased in rubber hose. 'And it won't dent you,' I added.

There were rough, wooden seats to either side, but I took up a position behind the cage so that I could watch both the clay and his action. Again I was sure that I was missing something. I hauled my mind back and paid attention. He missed the first one behind, then caught up and missed the next in front. I made him move his feet for better balance and reminded him to point and swing even as he was mounting the gun. He broke two and missed the next over.

'You didn't have your cheek down on the comb,' I said. 'Is it giving you a kick in the face?'

He rubbed his cheek thoughtfully. 'No, not really.'

'Then forget it and keep your head down. But never mind. You're getting it. Unload and come out of there. We'll change targets.'

The same house had a second trap which threw the clay up and away. I changed plugs and showed him the button to press for pairs. I have always found Springing Teal comparatively easy. I broke two pairs and then put him back in the cage.

'Pull up through them and, again, fire as you go past,' I said. 'I'll give you singles at first.'

He was a quick learner with good co-ordination, but he blew some holes in the empty air before he learned how to judge the climb of them. When he was hitting two out of three, I called a halt and coiled down the electric lead. 'Gather up the empties,' I said, 'and we'll skip to the tower.'

'Yes, ma'am,' he said.

I led the way again, but I had gone only a few yards when my thoughts came together and I stopped so suddenly that he bumped into me from behind. 'GC!' I said. 'Sorry,' I added.

'That's all right,' he said. 'I enjoyed it.'

His remark threw me. Perish the thought, but I was probably blushing. And he seemed surprised at himself for allowing the words to escape from him unprompted. It took several seconds before my thoughts sorted themselves out again.

'I was just thinking that there seemed to be fewer wads and broken clays lying around than I'd have expected,' I said. 'Most of them get scooped up by the grass-cutter. Grass doesn't grow much when it's dry at this time of year, but it seems to me that the place looks tidier than it did on Sunday. That's what the GC is in the diary. Grass-cutting. They must have a contractor who comes in once a fortnight in summer, on Mondays when the club's supposed to be shut.'

We were walking again and he had fallen into step beside me. He had to shorten his pace to match mine. He pushed back his ear-protectors in order to hear me better, although the high-tech ones are designed to allow speech to come through with very little distortion. 'Well done!' he said. 'You must be right.'

My mind still had the throttle wide open. 'What's more, I bet the same contractor does the Leisure Complex and the golf course,' I said. 'They were working there on Tuesday, remember? If he had two clients up here, it would make sense to do them on consecutive days.'

We had slowed to a halt in front of the tower, too engrossed to think where to walk. 'The diary entry was for the morning,' he said slowly. 'But I suppose the contractor might have needed most of the afternoon before he finished. He may have seen a visitor. But the pathologist put the death at evening up until midnight.'

'You're missing the point,' I said, 'which is that we've got a blank canvas. The grass-cutter would either pick up wads and throw them into the sort of hopper thing along with the grass-cuttings, or chop them up small – which is what it mostly does with the broken clays – they're only made of pitch and they're designed to be fragile – or it would tread them into the ground with the roller.' I stepped onto the grass and retrieved half of a plastic wad. 'Like this. So we have a sort of blank canvas, dating from whenever the grass-cutting finished.'

The Sergeant managed to look both pleased and disappointed. 'Just as I was getting my eye in!' he said. 'Perhaps we can resume later on. They have a lot more grass next door. Will you be all right on your own here while I go and see if the grass-cutter's still working?'

I refrained from pointing out that I had a gun in my hands. That sort of reasoning is not favoured by policemen, in whose philosophy only the criminal should be armed. 'I'll be fine,' I said. 'Lock your gun in the safe before you go. I'll take a look round.'

'Don't shoot and don't let anybody else shoot until I come back.'

I waited and looked him in the eye until he added the word, 'please.' Then I nodded. There are times and places for being masterful and he was not going to get away with jumping the gun – even if he had only been re-asserting himself.

I kept an eye cocked and an ear open, but it was still too early for shooters to arrive and the low-key publicity seemed to have been successful in putting the media off the scent. My search did not take long – I knew where wads were likely to collect from the various stands and I was familiar enough with their appearance for them to catch my eye.

There was no sign of the Sergeant when I unlocked the clubhouse. I filled and started up the coffee machine, checked the stores and phoned the week's orders to the suppliers.

That seemed to exhaust my duties for the moment. My watch and my stomach combined to assure me that it was lunchtime, although the morning seemed to have slipped away unnoticed. There were still a few sandwiches sealed in polythene. They felt fresh but they must have been about a week old. I decided to pass them up. I got two TV dinners out of the freezer, changed my mind and put one of them back, microwaved the other and ate it.

Like Dad, I hate to hang about like washing on a line. (His expression for it is more graphic but much less polite.) Casting around for something to do, I remembered the gun that Wallace had brought me for overhaul. The tools that Mr Tullos had used for his muzzle-loaders were in the office. There was a set of good screwdrivers – 'turnscrews', to the trade – a small clamp for V-springs and one of those useful things like an inkrubber impregnated with some abrasive compound.

I spread some outdated posters over one of the clubroom tables. When the Sergeant came back at last I had the gun stripped and was scrubbing away at a fine mask of rust. Some people shouldn't be allowed to own a good gun.

'There are some sandwiches left,' I said. 'Or I could heat you up something. On the house,' I added. 'And there's tea, coffee or soup in the machine.'

He laughed. 'I wish I'd known you were going to be so hospitable. I had something while I was hanging around at the Country Club. The tractormen had vanished to some secret hideaway to eat their "pieces".' He had resumed his suit jacket for the important business of seeing witnesses.

He slipped it off, hung it over the back of the chair, sat down and bent over my work. 'So that's what the insides look like!'

'They shouldn't, but some of them do.'

He watched my hands on the small components for a minute. 'You were right,' he said. 'Same firm, and the grass was cut on Monday. The Leisure Centre and the golf course take most of the rest of the week. And they say that Mr Tullos was giving somebody a lesson on the lower level while they were working up above. B. Torry, presumably.'

'Brian,' I said. 'Brian Torry.'

He nodded. 'They finished and left around five. Nobody was here then.'

'I had a look round while you were guzzling among the nobs at the Country Club,' I said. 'I found three different sorts of wads. I lifted one of each.' I took them out of the pocket of my Skeet jacket and put them on the table. 'The fibre wad is a twenty-bore, probably Eley to match the cartridges in the bin. It had been fired somewhere near the tower, I think at left-to-right crossers. This one—' I pushed a plastic wad across '—comes from one of the club's ordinary twelve-bore cartridges and it was on the Ball-trap layout. The last one is nineteen-millimetre G-wad from an Express cartridge. The mid-section's quite distinctive. It was below the Skeet layouts.'

'So three people came and shot here that evening?'

'Probably two,' I said. 'Possibly only one. A keen shot may use different cartridges or even a different gun for different disciplines. You may be able to work it out when you've studied the firing-pin marks on those cartridges, but you may not. Mr Tullos could have lent his own gun to a visitor. He used the club's cartridges when he was practising, but he sometimes used something more expensive when he had a bet on. I'd better come and show you where I found them.'

'Draw me a sketch map if you'd rather get on with polishing up those bits and pieces.'

90

'No,' I said. 'There's something else I want to show you.'

He sighed and got to his feet. 'I'm doing more mileage on this case than I've done in years! I had to chase those damned tractors all over the golf course.'

'We can take the guns along and finish your lesson,' I said.

He brightened slightly. 'That's different,' he said.

He bought another box of cartridges and I locked the clubhouse carefully. He fetched a camera from his car.

'Another thing,' I said, as we descended the steps. 'I wondered where the acoustic release had got to.'

'That's the thing you use when you're practising on your own?' he asked doubtfully. 'It makes the trap throw a . . . a bird when you call out?'

'That's it. I couldn't find it. So I took a look round. It was coiled up and locked in the Ball-trap trap-house.'

He stopped dead. 'Remember that you're talking to an ignoramus. What's a Ball-trap? A trap that throws a ball?'

I kept a straight face. 'It's one of the going-away disciplines, but the direction of the bird varies both sideways and up-and-down. The Continentals love it. It's not so well known here. It's sometimes laid on for visiting Americans.'

'They like it?'

'They've never seen it before,' I said. 'It breaks their hearts.'

'That's vicious,' said the Sergeant.

SEVEN

I showed him the wads. Those at the Ball-trap layout were widely scattered, as would be expected at a trap which oscillated to give random variations of angle in both planes. The twenty-bore wads were grouped as if the shooter had been practising on the very clays which we had found unbroken. The Express wads below the Skeet layouts were in two tidy arcs.

'This boy's good at Skeet,' I told the Sergeant.

'How can you tell?' he asked, exasperated.

'He takes the first of a pair early, reverses his swing and takes the second in the same place. And he shoots his singles just as consistently. Less skilled shots chase their birds all over the place.'

The Sergeant laid down his gun. I dawdled about, following up random thoughts, while he drew careful sketch-maps. 'For all the use this'll be in evidence. . .' he said. 'If these wads turn out to be relevant, the best evidence will be yours. But I'll try putting a paper flag over each of them and photographing each scene. . .'

'Before you do that,' I said, 'there's something else.' I led him to a position behind the nearest cage.'

'This layout's confusing me,' he said. 'Is this where we found the cartridges on Tuesday?'

The logic of the layout was so familiar to me that I had difficulty in realising that the network of paths and stands, which followed no geometric rules, could confuse the stranger. 'Correct. Now look.' I pointed out a deep spike-hole in the turf. 'I haven't seen any other imprints like this. I'd guess that foot-traffic plus the roller they hitch on behind the mowers would close them up.'

He squatted down and studied it carefully. 'Three questions,' he said. 'One, what made it? Two, why is it significant? And, three, how did you come to spot it under the blades of grass?'

He had looked up from the grass but not so far as to meet my eye. I could only think that he was studying my legs. I didn't mind. I am not ashamed of having legs, nor of the shape of them. 'Taking three first,' I said, 'I've been thinking over what people do here and what traces they leave behind. Skipping back to your first question, some of the older shooters, or the ones who have hip or back problems—'

'Such as the late Mr Tullos?'

'—take a shooting-stick round with them,' I said, persevering despite his interruption and the distraction of his study of my lower limbs. 'At most of the stands there's a wooden seat to each side, back out of the line of fire, but those seats get green and nasty in damp weather. And a coach who's giving a lesson, or someone who wants to see exactly how somebody else is getting it right or wrong, places himself behind the gun. Not too closely in line or you can't see the shot in the air —'

'Is that possible?' he asked incredulously.

'Anybody with quick vision can see it,' I said, 'except for the shooter, whose vision's masked by hot and expanding gases. For a high bird, you're better to be rather low. If you're almost but not quite in line behind him, you can watch the shooter out of the corner of your eye but focus on the clay. You see a grey blur go whisking past it. Between the two pictures, you can tell exactly what he's doing wrong. That's what I was doing behind you earlier.'

He looked up at my face. 'You think that Mr Tullos was giving a lesson after the grass-cutting finished?'

I raised my arms and let them fall in a sort of shrug.

'He used to use a sort of folding stool which doubled as a walking-stick,' I said. You're the detective. You figure it out.'

'The bent-tube thing? It was leaning against the gun-safe. Hang on a wee minute. I dare say that the exercise is doing me good.'

He dashed off. I stood where I was. Even in the dry weather the seats were rather grubby for a white cotton skirt. He came back shortly with Mr Tullos's stool in his hand.

'Was this the stool he used?'

'That's the one.' I appropriated it and sat down.

'It wouldn't mark the grass in dry weather.' He sighed. 'As you say, I'm the detective. I suppose it's up to me to figure out how we came to find twelve-bore cartridges and twenty-bore wads. Or do you have any more inspirations?'

'My inspirations are all used up for today,' I told him. 'Ask me again tomorrow.'

I sat and absorbed the warmth of the sun while he bustled about, lifting each wad and replacing it on a half-page from a notebook. He must have used half a roll of film in ensuring that the scene was recorded in his remarkably expensive camera. Either the camera was police property or he made thrifty use of his police pay. I noticed that he was managing to include me in several of the shots. I stood up, smiled and took up a glamorous pose, skirt slightly raised.

'Don't do that,' he said, smiling. 'This film will be developed in the police lab and I wouldn't like to think of the technician lusting over it. He's a married man.' The Sergeant's words were weighted to confirm that he himself was single. I noticed that he had taken the photograph before he spoke out.

I had been aware of the sound of a car on the road. Now I heard it turn in at the Gun Club's gates. 'We seem to be in business,' I said. 'You'd better get your little markers out of

94

sight if you don't want your cover blown. Is that the proper expression?'

He pulled a face. 'It's the proper expression if you're writing a TV script.' He began to pick up his paper flags.

I climbed the steps. Like Sergeant Fellowes, I was getting plenty of exercise.

Beside the jeep was parked a very swish BMW. It was no mere standard model, but one from the very top of the range which had then been taken to a specialist for another umpteen thousand to be spent on it.

Outside the locked clubhouse doors, a man was standing. He was looking around in the manner of one who has strayed out of safe and familiar territory. When I appeared with an open shotgun hooked over my arm, he looked almost scared. He was in his thirties, handsome in a wavy-haired, tooth-flashing way which set my teeth on edge. Something in his body language suggested to me that if he had not had something heavy on his mind he would have made a pass . . . and, I decided, would have got his face slapped for his pains.

'I take it that you're not a member,' I said.

'No,' he said. 'I . . . I'm looking for Sergeant Fellowes. You wouldn't be . . . ?'

'No, I wouldn't. But he'll be here in a jiffy.'

The Sergeant arrived a few seconds later, breathing heavily. His time for gathering up scraps of paper and climbing a flight of steps would have qualified him for the *Guinness Book of Records*.

When he saw another shotgun, my visitor took a step backwards and looked around him – wondering, no doubt, what sort of police operation he had strayed into. When he saw no signs of a siege, his nerve came back. 'I'm Basil Chambers,' he said.

'Sergeant Fellowes,' said Sergeant Fellowes. 'We'd better go inside.'

Mr Chambers must be the witness who had visited the noise attenuation banking on the day of the murder, and I was aching to hear what he had to say. But another car, a nearly new Jag in a pleasing shade of green, was turning in at the gates. If this standard was kept up, I thought, we would soon be as up-market as the Country Club next door. Duty, if not already calling, seemed to be clearing its throat.

'Sit in one of the cars,' I said. 'Or go into the house. There are people coming.'

The Sergeant handed me his gun and got into the BMW. I unlocked the clubroom and was waiting at the bar, which doubled as the business desk, before the three men from the Jag walked in. I had seen all their faces before at some time in the past, but if I had ever known their names I had forgotten them. The two who arrived in the lead must have been in their fifties and each had the sort of self-confidence which comes from security and a set place in the world.

'I know that you're Miss Calder, because I've seen you shooting here,' the first said. He was a benign-looking man, rather puckish, with a balding head but a fine set of whiskers to make up for it. Sir Peter had said that he was in whisky wholesaling. 'Peter Hay phoned to say that you were going to keep things going until somebody else was appointed. Sad about Herbert Tullos, wasn't it?'

'Very,' I said.

His companion nodded mournfully. He was taller, grey-haired and slightly stooping and he looked as though he had never smiled in his life. 'Peter said something about an accident. But the police have been asking questions, so it seems that they haven't closed the file. What exactly happened? Not a shooting accident, was it?'

'Not as far as I know,' I said. 'You're both members, aren't you?'

Enough had been said about the defunct steward. They produced their membership cards. The smaller man with

96

the whiskers was James Torrance while the taller with the gloomy expression was Oliver Gray.

The third member of the party came forward, a thickset man in his thirties. 'Charles Aiken,' he said and waited.

'Member?' I asked. Then I gave myself a mental kick up the backside and told myself to think more carefully before succumbing to the habit of verbal shorthand. My enquiry might well have been taken for an invitation to lay his member on the counter between us.

He nodded, but behind his back Mr Torrance was grinning and shaking his head. 'May I see your card?' I asked.

He felt in his pockets. 'I seem to have left it at home,' he said. His accent was broader than that of the other two and he was wearing jeans as against their serviceable but tailor-made slacks. His manner was brash, but some people carry anxiety around with them, exuding it like body odour, and he was one of them.

'Then I'm afraid you'll have to pay for a day-membership,' I said. 'Or will you wait while I look for the list of members?'

He hesitated and then shrugged. 'I'll pay,' he said. 'The club can do with the extra cash.'

This was patently nonsense but I let it go and took his money. They stocked up with cartridges.

'Rambo and I have a bet,' Oliver Gray said sadly. It came back to me that he always called his friend 'Rambo' as a form of inverted humour. Anybody less like a macho killer than the small and gnomelike James Torrance would have been hard to imagine. 'Twenty Ball-trap. We're taking our wives to France next month and the French don't seem to go in for anything else. Then we met Charlie and he asked if he could come along. Do you want to take a corner of the bet, Charlie?'

Mr Aiken hesitated and then said that he supposed so.

'How about yourself?' Mr Gray asked me. 'Tenner a head.'

Backing myself against the members and visitors, a girl would be on a hiding to nothing. If I lost I would be losing money I could not afford, while if I won they would never forgive me. 'I have a pupil under instruction,' I said. 'He can shoot with you, if he wants to and if you don't mind, but I'm not having him take any bets until I've brought him up to scratch.' I glanced regretfully at the dismantled gun on the table. 'I'll come and score for you until he's ready.'

'Fair enough.' Rambo Torrance had followed my eyes. 'I forgot you were Keith's daughter. In the business, aren't you? My game gun needs an overhaul and the trigger-pulls adjusted. Care to take it on?'

'Any time,' I said.

There was a stack of blank score-cards under the bar. They kitted themselves out and collected their guns. Mr Torrance had an over-under Miroku trap-gun; Charles Aiken a Japanese over-under. Oliver Gray carried a side-by-side game gun of undoubted quality. I carried Sergeant Fellowes's cartridges and the gun which he had been using and we set off down to the lower level.

They took up positions on the row of marker slabs, each with a construction like a small bird-table in front of it for cartridges. They would move one place to the right after each had had one shot, so that after five shots apiece they would each have shot from every position and be back where they started. I switched on the ball-trap and in the low trap-house in front of them it began its rather human bowing and scraping movements.

Sergeant Fellowes came down to join us a minute or two later. He caught my eye and combined a wink with a shrug.

'Just stand and watch for a minute,' I told him. We stepped back slightly, so that we could chat without ear-protectors and without disturbing the shooters' concentration. James Torrance called. I released a standard clay and he hit it with his second barrel. 'Loss, kill,' I said. 'Don't

98

rush your shot,' I told the Sergeant, 'but you can't hang about too long or the target's out of range. You score three for a first barrel kill, two for a second barrel. What did he say?' I added in a whisper.

'Very little.'

'But what?'

'Tell you later.'

I had missed Charles Aiken's call. I apologised and concentrated on the serious business of competition.

The Sergeant said that he was ready to try himself out. He went forward and took up a vacant position. His co-ordination and his quick reactions stood him in good stead and Ball-trap seemed to suit his style. He was averaging three for five shots by the time the other three had finished. Rambo Torrance collected his winnings. His score was not spectacular, but Oliver Gray was handicapped by an unsuitable gun and Charles Aiken seemed over-eager. They picked up their empty cartridges and dropped them into the bin without being asked.

'Does anybody fancy making more contributions to my early retirement fund?' Mr Torrance asked. 'Or shall we try some Sporting?'

'Sporting for me,' Aiken said. 'I never was any good at going-away birds and my gun's too open-choked for them.'

'I'll knock off now and have a coffee or something,' Oliver Gray said glumly. 'My shoulder's beginning to feel pulverised.'

'The trap at the far end's set for Springing Teal,' I said. 'Will that do for the moment? Trap for yourselves, I'll have to go and open the clubhouse again.'

The Sergeant glanced once at the bin, which now held sample cartridges from three guns plus two sets of finger-prints. (Mr Torrance, as was his habit, was shooting in thin gloves.) But the Sergeant's eye was bright with the light of dawning enthusiasm. 'I – er – I think I'll just tag along and use up the rest of my cartridges,' he said. 'Is that all right?'

'Just don't go making any bets on yourself,' I said. 'You're not yet up to matching yourself against these sharks.' The Sergeant seemed disappointed, but the other two looked flattered.

I climbed the steps again beside Oliver Gray and unlocked the clubhouse for him. I was half inclined to go down again and rejoin my pupil, in whom I was taking a professional interest. (At least, I hoped that it was mostly professional. I mostly hoped that his interest in me was not.) But even if he had learned something of interest from his visitor, he would be difficult to detach from the others while he could be pursuing his new interest.

Mr Gray bought himself a low alcohol lager and I accepted a shandy. 'If your gun hurts your shoulder,' I said, 'are you sure that it fits you?'

He blinked at me. 'I think so,' he said. 'Had it for years. It never bothers me at a game shoot.'

I got him to stand and mount the unloaded gun so that I could check the fit. It seemed adequate. I weighed the gun in my hands. 'It's very light,' I said. Privately, I thought that the club's cut-price cartridges (loaded in Taiwan) contributed to the recoil problem, but Wal would never have forgiven me if I had said so. 'You need a bit more weight to mop up the recoil when you're shooting clays – you fire more shots in quick succession and you don't have to carry it very far. And if you're going to mix disciplines you'd be better with a choice of chokes. You're giving your friends an unfair advantage. It's up to yourself, of course, but we've a gun in the shop that might suit you very well.'

His glum expression brightened very slightly. 'Could I try it?'

'Of course,' I said.

'Bring it on Saturday and I'll see if it does anything for me.'

If Oliver Gray was prepared to spend anything from a few hundred to a thousand or more in the hope of winning occasional fivers, who was I to deter him when I would cheerfully have done the same? You can't put a price on the thrill of victory. It only remained to see what we had in the shop. There ought to be something. I thought that I was getting to be as big a rogue as Dad.

We had remained standing while we discussed guns, but Mr Gray gave a faint groan and subsided into a chair. 'Excuse me,' he said. 'My hips keep telling me that they've carried too much weight too far and too often over the years.'

He had taken a seat beside the table with the dismantled gun on it. I sat down and resumed my cleaning operation. 'You should use a shooting stick,' I said impulsively. I thought that I might sell him one along with a new gun. A man who would jib at treating himself to a moderately expensive gift is often more willing to add that amount to a larger cheque.

'I do, sometimes,' he said, 'at the Sporting stands, where you fire ten and then stand and wait. Not for Ball-trap or Down the Line, when you're shooting every few seconds. Rambo's hips are worse than mine, but he won't give in and sit down. Thinks it's a confession of old age, I suppose. Perhaps it is. On the other hand, it's convenient being a sort of grandfather figure, when you're as lazy as I am.'

'What rubbish!' I said. Although he still had a tired-bloodhound look, I thought that, inside, he was laughing at himself and poking fun at the world.

'Perhaps,' he said with the faintest suggestion of a smile. 'But every day it comes closer to being true.' We were quiet for a minute. The shots outside were no more than a distant popping. I could not believe that the noise seriously bothered the would-be nobs in the timeshare units. As if reading my thoughts, he said, 'Tell me, has that crook McGruer from next door been lobbying you yet about their offer to buy the club? You know about that?'

'He was here this morning, wanting to know whether I'd have a seat on the committee.'

'And you told him . . . ?'

'That I didn't know and that any offer wouldn't be a matter for the committee but for the whole membership.'

Mr Gray looked gloomier than ever. 'Quite right. He knew it, but you were right to remind him. The trouble is that most of the active members are on the committee. Others have moved away or gone abroad. They keep up their membership because that's much cheaper than rejoining if and when they return. Others have given it up and taken to basket-making. There are a few life-members tucked away in homes for the elderly. So the active membership's down to the hard-core few. The entrance fee's too stiff for most pockets.'

'Because of the value of the land and assets,' I said.

'Exactly. Outright planning consent adds a few thou' to the value,' he said. 'If the membership decide to sell up and share out the money instead of re-establishing the club, there'll be a nice little windfall for each of us.'

It hadn't occurred to me that there might be serious danger of the offer being accepted. 'They won't, will they?' I asked.

'They might. Nobody's immune to the lure of lucre if you catch him just when his business needs a fresh injection of cash or his wife's demanding new furniture. And there are other clubs to join. The old order changeth. Herb Tullos was dead . . .' He stopped with a wry look. 'I'm sorry, I'll rephrase that. He was set against it and now he's gone. Two new members were elected only last week – cash on the barrel, as they say, without even having visited the place to find out whether they enjoyed it or not. I strongly suspect that they were put up to it by our friend McGruer. And Charlie Aiken, who tried to kid you that he was a member, has applied for membership. Peter Hay's stalling, just in case he's another quisling.'

'I heard that Mr Tullos was about to change his tune,' I said.

'Was he, by God! That makes it interesting. So he

102

could have been whacked on the head by anybody – like myself – who was against a takeover, or by somebody who was for it and didn't know that he was about to turn his coat. Such things can happen over much less when tempers flare up.'

'How did you know that he was whacked on the head?' I asked him.

For the only time in our acquaintanceship, he actually laughed. 'Peter Hay told me. He asked me to keep it under my hat, but I seem to have slipped.'

'I'm sorry,' I said.

'You're forgiven. Don't forget to ask Peter to confirm it.'

Mr Gray watched for a minute as I oiled a leaf mainspring and coaxed it back into place. When the risk of it slipping out of the clamp and shooting into a corner of the room was over, he spoke again, more vehemently. 'If it happens, I can't bear the thought of starting off again in some club with fewer facilities – no clubhouse, and nothing but DTL and English Sporting – and a lot of keen young members who think they're God's gift to sport.'

'Mr McGruer said that they'd be keeping the place open,' I said.

He snorted derisively. 'They've got some timeshare units unsold. If they can turn the place into a whizzbang commercial enterprise – big-money sponsored competitions, Starshot, television deals and all that jazz – they'll sell the rest of the units or be able to rent them out as accommodation for competitors. There'll be no place for the likes of Rambo and me. The relaxed and friendly atmosphere will be gone.'

'I didn't see much relaxation or friendship at the Ball-trap this afternoon,' I said.

He patted my hand in a way that was not wholly fatherly. 'You sell me the right gun and get me winning with it, and I'll relax and be so friendly that you won't recognise me,' he said.

EIGHT

By the time the three men finished shooting and came to join us in the clubhouse, I had reassembled the gun and tested the trigger-pulls.

'Finished?' Mr Gray asked as I slipped it into its sleeve.

'All but the strikers,' I said. 'I need a tool to take out the discs. These are the tools Mr Tullos used for his muzzle-loaders.'

'No discs,' he said, nodding.

The men were hungry, but showed every intention of staying on for the evening session. The Sergeant seemed to have melted in among them, almost unnoticed.

Catering at the Pentland Gun Club was of the simplest, calculated to be managed by one steward with occasional help from the club's office-bearers in times of stress. Low alcohol drinks were on sale, with stronger liquor available at the steward's discretion. A tea and coffee dispenser murmured to itself against one wall. For the rest, anything which could not be stored in a freezer and readied in a microwave oven or a toasting sandwich-maker was unavailable and that was that. Visitors could like it, lump it or bring their own.

I palmed off the last of those wrapped sandwiches on them as a sort of outsize *hors d'oeuvre* while they waited and then dished up a meal of chicken portions and vegetables followed by ice cream. They paid the modest menu price without grumbling.

Rambo Torrance, who seemed to have taken a fancy to me, was complimentary. 'We'll have to continue with lady stewards,' he said. 'Tullos's chicken always came out like rubber.'

'You'd prefer the female of the species because they can't shoot better than you can,' Oliver Gray said.

My hackles rose; and Rambo, with his whiskers seeming to stand on end, looked much less puckish. 'That's fighting talk,' he said. 'We'll have to see whether your money goes where your mouth is.'

We were in the middle of eating when a new-looking small car rolled up to the door.

'First of the evening gang,' Mr Gray said.

'And probably the last,' Rambo Torrance said. 'Thursdays are usually quiet. Most of them won't know that the club's back in business.'

We all knew, at least by sight, the blonde woman who had driven the car. Gertrude Cowan was a likeable but rather vulgar widow in her thirties, with an accent which could have diced carrots and a figure which seemed to be attractive to men although I thought it overblown. She wore the universal Skeet vest and cap, but over a dress which would have got by at a garden party. She had originated in Glasgow but now lived on the outskirts of Newton Lauder. Her late husband, who had left her more than adequately provided for, had first brought her clay-busting some years before and she had taken to it with enthusiasm if not with real skill. After his death she had continued to make occasional visits – more, I thought, for the sake of the male company than for the sport.

Her companion was a dark and rather skinny woman of about the same age, who was introduced as Mrs Hickson – Beatrice to friends. She was demure in dress and looks. I remembered seeing her shooting DTL, quite competently. She had been in the company of a husband who suffered the twin handicaps of a very loud voice and an inability to remember the first rules of safe gun-handling, so I was relieved that they had come . . . whatever may be the female equivalent of 'stag'.

105

The ladies had not eaten. I was obliged to abandon my own meal in order to cook for them. From behind the bar, I could pick up the threads of the conversation.

'We knew that there'd been an accident, of course,' Mrs Hickson was saying. 'But I could hear shooting this afternoon. Derek's away at some golf tournament so I phoned Gertrude.'

I tried to catch the Sergeant's eye but he was keeping his head down over his plate.

'And I said all right, let's shoot a round of Skeet and see what's going on,' Mrs Cowan said.

'Is something going on?' Mr Gray asked. He was seated facing me but he avoided my eye.

'She means about the death of Mr Tullos,' Mrs Hickson explained. 'The Scottish News almost said that it was an accident. But they didn't quite say it and they didn't say that the police were satisfied, as they usually do. And there were policemen all over the place for the first day or so.'

'They've been going round the members and the more regular visitors,' Mr Torrance said, 'asking us when we were last here and what we were doing on Monday evening.'

Mrs Cowan nodded her over-bright golden head. 'They suspect a murder,' she said. 'How exciting! They haven't got to me yet, and I'm a member – but I've only just got back from a visit to my brother in Inverness. I expect they'll come and find me tomorrow.' She sounded hopeful.

'I haven't heard from them either,' Mr Aiken said. 'But this is my first visit here in a month. I was working with my accountant on Monday evening and we've got a year's accounts to show for it. We went for a drink afterwards.'

'It's your accountant's job to back you up,' Mrs Hickson said.

'This one hates my guts. I think he's on the side of the tax inspector.'

'I was here on Sunday,' Mrs Cowan said. 'Beatrice couldn't get away.' I was putting two more meals onto plates. She turned her head to look at me. 'So were you,

106

dear, on Sunday, weren't you? Monday evening, I was out with a gentleman friend.'

Rambo Torrance chuckled. 'From the questions the police were asking, they want to know what people were doing up to midnight. When did you part from your gentleman friend?'

'That's none of your business,' Mrs Cowan said coyly. 'If the police ask me, I shan't keep anything back and never mind what they think! What did you tell them? And what were you really doing?'

Mr Gray snorted without mirth. 'Rambo and I are partners,' he said. 'And we're both fancy-free. We do most things together. We've satisfied the police as to what we were doing on Monday night and if we can satisfy them . . . we should be able to satisfy anybody else.'

(I looked at him out of the corner of my eye and then at the Sergeant. Earlier, Mr Gray had mentioned wives; but now he was hinting at satisfaction for all comers. Evidently out of sight was out of mind.)

'I was only making conversation,' Mrs Cowan said stiffly. His *double entendre* seemed to have passed her by.

Rambo hurried to make amends. 'We were here a week ago,' he said. 'Don't mind Oliver. He doesn't like being puzzled and he can't understand – neither of us can – why the police were interested in our guns. They weren't handing out any information, but as far as we know there's been no suggestion that Herb Tullos was shot. Yet they came round with a boxful of primed cartridges. Not loaded, you understand, just with a live primer in. And they popped them off, once for each barrel, and put them in envelopes just as if they'd been found at the scene of a crime.'

'That's weird,' Mr Aiken said.

I brought the ladies' food to the table and resumed my own now cold meal. The police had chosen the easiest way to obtain firing-pin impressions from the witnesses' guns, but firing primed but unloaded cases was not going to give them impressions of the breech-faces. I wondered

107

whether anybody had ever fooled the police by swapping firing-pins between guns. With many modern production guns, it would be too easy.

The Sergeant, although listening with a concentration which made me think that he was memorising every word, had never lifted his eyes off his empty plate. Beatrice Hickson, when she had glanced round the table, had avoided looking in his direction. I was more than ever sure that she was the witness who had been up on the embankment on Monday night, that the Sergeant knew it and that she knew of both his knowledge and his identity. But the demure Mrs Hickson with the flashily handsome Basil Chambers, all teeth and sideburns! How could she? I reminded myself that, to judge from the freaks you see pushing prams, sexual attraction follows some surprising paths.

Temptation was too much for me. 'I was shooting rabbits with my uncle on Monday evening,' I said. 'So my alibi's as good as anybody's. What were you doing?' I asked her as casually as I could manage.

She shot me a look from under lowered eyelids, a look which the microwave oven could hardly have improved on. She knew that my question was barbed. She was not the type to make brazen admissions. On the other hand, she could guess that a blank evasion would only encourage me to probe further. 'I watched the telly for most of the evening,' she said slowly. 'But, later on, I did take a walk in this direction. I heard some shots, that was all.'

In strictly literal terms, that could have been true. 'Any particular pattern of shots?' I asked. The different disciplines produce quite different variations in the timing of shots. And in their loudness, because a shot fired away from the listener sounds much softer than one fired in his direction.

She looked at me again and this time her glance was thoughtful. 'I never thought about it before,' she said, 'but,

108

yes. The pattern was . . . I think whoever it was was one man shooting Skeet.'

'What fun!' Gertrude Cowan said brightly. She had been in skittish mood ever since she had gathered that the two friends were unencumbered. 'It's like being a detective. Did you see anything?'

Beatrice Hickson shook her dark head. She had admitted as much as she was prepared to admit. 'I . . . I didn't come all the way,' she said.

Whether it was said in innocence or this was another shattering *double entendre* I could not tell, but I saw that Sergeant Fellowes was fighting against a huge laugh which was building up inside him. I struggled to hide my own giggles.

'How very disappointing,' I said.

Rambo at least recognised the undercurrent in the conversation. He was quick to offer a change of subject. 'Herb Tullos was against a sell-out,' he said. 'I wonder how the voting would go now.'

'If the offer was enough to replace the clubhouse and all the doodahs on another site,' Mrs Cowan said, 'plus a nice little bonus for all the members. . . well, why not? This place will be haunted. Mr Tullos was just the sort of person whose ghost would hang around and put people off.' She paused and looked thoughtful. 'You'd think that the police would be haunting the place too,' she said.

Beatrice Hickson said nothing but she flicked a glance at Sergeant Fellowes.

Mr Torrance broke into a short silence. 'You mentioned Skeet,' he said. 'That sounds good. If nobody else turns up, why don't we have a round of Skeet?'

'Not for me,' said Aiken. 'I can't shoot Skeet worth a damn. I'll get some more practice at Ball-trap if that's all right? And next time out I'll clobber the lot of you.'

'The acoustic release is hanging in the trap-house,' I

said. 'Pay me for your birds before you go. And I want day-membership money from Mrs Hickson and bird-money all round.'

Nobody likes parting with money, but the mood soon revived. 'That leaves three of each,' Rambo said. 'Why don't we have a team match? Ladies against gents? Or mixed doubles, three teams, each of one M and one F, twenty-five birds each? Fiver a head?'

'I'm a rank beginner,' the Sergeant said nervously. 'I've never even seen Skeet, let alone shot it.'

'And Miss Calder's the pro,' Rambo retorted. 'We'll team you together and credit you with three birds between you before we start. How about that?'

There was an avaricious glint in his usually jolly eye, and but for Mr Gray's earlier remark I would have backed off, pointing out that I was officially the steward, not the coach and definitely not the pro. But, thinking it over, I remembered that Mrs Hickson's only proven talent was at DTL, I had only seen Mrs Cowan attempting Skeet without conspicuous success, Rambo Torrance's Miroku was a less than perfect fit while Oliver Gray's sidelock had fixed and rather tight chokes. And they were each stocked up with the club's standard cartridges. These were loaded with very hard shot which in most guns could be counted on to pattern well but rather tightly. On the other hand, Skeet was my favourite discipline. I enjoyed its predictability. From every station, in calm conditions, each bird could be counted on to maintain a precise course and speed, and, given practice and good reactions, there was nothing difficult about it. The Sergeant might get by. I hesitated.

'We're game,' Gertrude Cowan said. She looked me in the eye. 'But perhaps a fiver's too much for you?'

'Or aren't three birds enough?' Oliver Gray asked.

Beatrice Hickson smiled patronisingly. 'I don't think that you should be betting at your tender age,' she said. She gave a sudden and disconcertingly loud crack of laughter.

'You're on,' the Sergeant said firmly.

'Provided,' I put in, 'that I get half an hour to show him the rudiments first.'

I took the Sergeant through to the office and made him try the club's Winchester Skeet gun for fit.

'What in hell got into you?' I asked him. 'I could see that they were needling you.'

'I didn't mind. Well, not too much. I can take it. Men tend to resent girls who shoot. And women are always women.'

He stuck out his chin. 'Well, I didn't like it. I'll pay the fivers if we lose. But I don't think we will. I've seen you shoot.'

He had sounded genuinely concerned for me. For the first time in my life I could feel an exchange of sexual messages deep down at a subliminal level, and when, in checking the gun for fit, I touched his hand it was as intimate and personal as a brush of lips. 'Thanks for the vote of confidence,' I said lightly, 'but you haven't seen me shoot Skeet. Skeet can be difficult. When you go off form, you go right off. Stand still.' The stock of the Skeet gun was slightly short for him and would have bruised his fingers, but a slip-on butt-pad out of Herbert Tullos's cupboard gave him room and brought his eye nicely in line with the rib.

'Can't I use the gun I've spent all afternoon getting used to?' he asked unhappily.

'Totally unsuitable,' I said. 'It would be slow to swing and shoot slightly high.' I tapped the pair of shatterproof glasses in his breast pocket. 'You'll need these. In Skeet, the birds are taken close. Now, hold your horses.' I went through to the store-room and dug out some Skeet cartridges which Mr Tullos had kept on an inconspicuous shelf. On the way out, I called at the jeep for twenty-bore Skeet cartridges of my own.

'These may give us an edge,' I said as we walked to the Skeet layouts. 'Small shot, patterning wide. You'll see

111

why. If you can hit some of the singles and just one of each of the doubles, we may scrape through.'

All signs of the recent death and police activity had been removed from the first layout. 'Would it bug you to shoot on this one?' I asked him.

'Not a bit,' he said. 'Did you think I was going to trip over the memory of a body?' His smile was slightly grim. 'Let's see if it bothers anyone else.'

I was dying to ask him what the flashy Mr Chambers had said – especially about Beatrice Hickson – but I wanted his mind on his shooting. Besides, he had not proved very forthcoming with information and I was not seeking a snub. I showed him the birds and the sequence of shooting and let him try with dummy cartridges – 'snap caps' – in the gun. The speed of it daunted him at first, but when I let him try it for real his fast reactions came to his aid. By the time the others came out he had used up one box of cartridges and was hitting one single in three. He could make little of the doubles – which, at Skeet, are released simultaneously but in opposite directions, one high bird and one low, crossing near the centre of the semicircular layout. It was too early to expect it.

Rambo Torrance had paired with Gertrude Cowan – and not, I thought, because he had a preference for vulgar blondes. Oliver Gray brought his shooting-stick. He was the more competent of the two men, and Beatrice Hickson, although I had only seen her performing on going-away birds, looked confident. So the better two of our opponents had ganged up on us . . .

We tossed coins for precedence, odd team out to go first, and of course the Sergeant and I ended up with the doubtful honour. Ladies first, by general decision. I led the Sergeant to Station One, backing against the high trap-house. Rambo took the remote control release and I called for my first bird.

I powdered the two singles and at least chipped both

birds of the pair. Then I changed places with the Sergeant, who missed all four.

'Remember where I told you to take them,' I told him as gently as I could. 'Relax. And keep your head down.'

We moved to Station Two. Feeling irritated, because I knew that he could do better, I let one of the singles get away; he responded by breaking both of the singles.

In English Skeet, no doubles are shot on Stations Three and Five, so when we finished on Station Seven, right where Herbert Tullos had lain, we had fired 24 shots each. I had dropped another single and one of a pair, so I stood at 21. My partner had hit 7.

Unlike the American version, there is no Station Eight in the centre for English Skeet. Instead, the first bird to have been missed is taken again. I hit my single on Station Two and on Station One he blew his to smoke. Add our handicap of 3 and we had notched up 32; a passable score in the circumstances, but definitely beatable.

'I let you down,' he said.

'Not many do better at the first attempt,' I said. I could afford to be generous if he was going to pay up for both of us.

We stepped well back. Rambo Torrance and Gertrude Cowan took our places. Oliver Gray moved his shooting-stick and took the remote control to do duty as trapper.

I found myself standing with Beatrice Hickson. She was the least-known quantity. She was also the performer who would most probably determine whether we won or lost. Temptation began to rise in me like yeast. I do not usually play foul. The Skeet championship of the universe, if there is ever such a trophy, would not please my eye on my shelf if I had won it by the use of gamesmanship. But I had been manoeuvred into shooting, for money, partnered by a complete novice. Besides, her remarks were rankling.

'What did you really see on Monday evening?' I asked her.

She raised her painted eyebrows at me. 'Nothing. I

told you. I turned back long before I reached here.'

'That isn't quite what you said.'

'What did I say, then?' She sounded amused, as if by the antics of a child.

'That you "didn't come all the way". Rather a slur on poor Basil's performance, don't you think?'

Her eyebrows came down as if they'd been shot flying and white patches appeared on her nose and cheekbones. 'I don't know what you mean,' she said. She sounded very much less amused.

'I think you do,' I said. 'I think you came here to find out what was being said and done. You wanted to know what chance you had of the investigation rolling by without flattening you. What did you see?'

'Nothing.'

'What did you say your husband's name was?' I asked. 'Derek, wasn't it?'

'You wouldn't,' she said. She looked at my face. 'Christ, I believe you would! Is this just because I said that you were still a child?'

'You should have known better,' I said, with a smile which I hoped would be taken for cynical, 'at your age. What did you see from up there?' I nodded my head towards the embankment, although the safety walls cut off any view of it.

'I've already told the police. Derek was hardly down the road before there was an inspector at the door. At least they had the decency to wait until he was out of sight and to ask politely. They didn't resort to blackmail.'

'And now you can tell me.'

She stood and seethed for a minute before deciding that whatever she said would hardly alter her situation. 'Not a lot,' she said. 'A man's figure. He was coming back from down there, somewhere around the high tower. He seemed to be in a hurry. He disappeared around here, among the Skeet layouts. After that, I was a bit preoccupied.'

I looked round for the Sergeant, but he was busy. He was

114

standing by himself and doing something so casually that I almost missed it. He had recovered sample cartridges and was surreptitiously marking them. 'I bet you were,' I said. 'Did you see him leave?'

'I heard a car drive off, that's all.'

'Did you see it?'

'Not then. Earlier, I'd noticed a pale car standing beside the steward's old van.'

'What sort of car? And what sort of pale?'

'A saloon, I think. Or a hatchback. Not an estate, anyway. I couldn't tell you anything about the colour. The light was just going.'

'And the man? What did he look like?'

She shrugged. 'Just a man. I thought that it was the steward, Tullos or whatever his name was. He could have bought himself another car. God knows he needed it. And he could have afforded it, the bets he used to win.'

Gertrude and Rambo were finishing their round – on 28 between them, I gathered. Oliver Gray was beckoning Mrs Hickson. But she was recovering her temper, too soon. I wondered whether I dared suggest that she and her boy-friend had bopped Mr Tullos because he had played the Peeping Tom, and decided that I did not.

'How many others have you had it away with around here?' I softly asked her retreating back. Her stride checked. Then she walked on, but stiffly. That, I thought, should do it.

And so it proved. Mr Gray shot a 21, almost equalling my score; but Mrs Hickson was snatching at her shots and scored 9, well below her form and not much better than the Sergeant. Afterwards, she called me a little bitch under her breath as she coughed up her fiver.

Instead of patronising the club bar, the two ageing Romeos swept the ladies off for a drink at the Country Club. I decided that I need not bother to wish them luck and an exchange of herpes. Whatever their partners might think – and Mrs Cowan was already wagging her tail – the

115

men were too near their own doorsteps for more than an evening of flirtation.

They had quite forgotten about Mr Aiken, who returned from the Ball-trap just as the Jag vanished up the road and was none too pleased to find himself left behind.

'Don't you drive?' I asked him.

'Banned,' he said. 'Another six months to go. That's why I jump at any chance of a lift.' He handed me the acoustic release, paid for his clays and then stumped off towards the Country Club, to claim his lift home and, I hoped, to play gooseberry. I am usually tolerant and open-minded, but I was in a mood to find elderly and illicit amours distasteful.

Sergeant Fellowes remained. He helped me to pick up the unbroken clays and disposed of such empty cartridges as were surplus to the requirements of the police laboratory while I locked up the trap-houses and other gear.

Then there was peace. Uncle Ronnie had not cast up yet. I made up the books and then sat on the bench which was now getting the benefit of the evening sun, with the Sergeant beside me. I told him what Mrs Hickson had said.

He seemed amused. 'Is that why she was shooting so erratically? That's wicked. It's true what Kipling said about the female of the species. We knew most of that,' he added more soberly, 'but you've added a little something. The trouble is, it doesn't make sense yet.'

'What did Mr Chambers tell you?' I asked him.

'About Beatrice? He was embarrassingly explicit.'

'I didn't mean that,' I said, 'and you know it.'

'True.'

'I've told you everything and you don't tell me a damn thing,' I said sadly. 'Do you think I can't keep my mouth shut?'

He smiled at me so that his eyes wrinkled. 'You haven't shown much aptitude for it so far.'

I aimed a friendly slap at his leg. He caught my hand and

held onto it. 'Even a consultant doesn't get the whole story. Nobody does, usually, except the Investigating Officer and his immediate team. People let things slip, sometimes. So don't be hurt.' He gave my hand a little shake. 'I'll have to go in to a briefing tomorrow. Reporting by radio is all very well . . .'

'But there comes a time when you have to deliver your sample cartridges?'

'You noticed? I hope nobody else did.'

'Did you take some of my cartridges? I can always count them.'

'Yes, of course I did,' he said. 'Why should it bother you? You're innocent, aren't you?'

I knew that I was innocent. I could hardly say that I would have hoped that he needed no proof of my innocence. The law does not work that way. 'It doesn't bother me,' I said.

'I don't know what time I'll get out here again. Will you feel safe on your own?'

'I'm not the nervous type.'

'No, I don't think you are. I've enjoyed my day,' he said. But I saw a momentary look of reserve. (I was becoming adept at reading his expressions. I wondered what that new perceptiveness was a sign of.) 'I can understand the fun you get,' he said. 'I can imagine what it's like to win a cup. But you shoot real birds as well, don't you? Pheasants and things?'

'Now and again,' I said.

'Doesn't it bother you, killing something?'

'Sometimes. If I wing a bird and don't manage to gather it. Did you enjoy your chicken?'

He blinked at me, puzzled. 'It was good,' he said.

'Doesn't it ever bother you that your chicken, and your eggs, are produced in battery conditions by birds which never know life in the wild? Have you ever wondered what life would be like for a battery hen? Most people don't bother.'

'I've bothered. Perhaps not as often as I should.' From his tone, I knew that he really had bothered. He was an unusual policeman. Most police decide early that the letter of the law should take the place of conscience.

'Have you ever wished that we could turn them loose to grow up and breed in the wild and only recover them when they were needed for the table?'

He paused before answering. 'Not in so many words,' he said at last.

'Because that's what we do. And the birds which we recover are free range and absolutely without preservatives or colouring. What's your excuse?'

'My what?'

'You're a hunter too,' I pointed out.

'I suppose I am, in a way. Have we known each other long enough to exchange the stories of our lives?'

'Just bits,' I said.

'Then you may as well hear this bit.' He had been speaking lightly but now he was very serious. 'When I was young, I admired and respected my father very much. He was a god to me.

'One day he was attacked in the street, beaten up by a gang of youths for no reason except devilment.'

'I'm sorry,' I said. And I was sorrier than could be expressed in two words. Or two thousand.

'His injuries weren't serious. But the damage to his self-regard never quite healed. It was months before he'd even leave the house on his own. He made excuses. And even when he seemed to have got over it, I knew that he was wondering what his family thought of him now.

'I can't honestly tell you that I joined the police only because of that incident, or because I loathe and detest the arrogance that makes one man assume the right to attack another. But, deep inside me, I think that that was a large part of it. I still see my father often. You must meet him some day. I'm very fond of him, but he isn't a god any more. And whenever I meet up with violence, I remember.'

118

'I'm sorry,' I said again.

'It's water under the bridge now,' he said. 'Be careful tomorrow, until I come. And if anybody new turns up to shoot—'

'I'll keep a few cartridges and note who it was and what the gun was.'

'I was going to repeat, be careful. We've no more men to spare or I'd send somebody out—'

'To baby-sit?'

He smiled at me again from about six inches. Something seemed to be drawing our faces together. 'If the cap fits. But be as careful with your tongue as you would be with a shotgun. It could be just as dangerous.'

'Keep my mouth open and empty? I'll remember.'

He chuckled. 'Couldn't I help you to defrost that fridge?'

His mention of my tongue had made me very conscious of it, so that it seemed to fill my mouth. 'Janet said to bring you for a meal on Sunday evening. If you'd like.' Surely, I thought, this was how it should be, not a quick romp in the bushes with somebody else's spouse.

'I'd like that very much,' he said.

A door slammed. Our lips had just touched, very lightly. The Sergeant let go of my hand in a hurry and got to his feet. I heard the jeep's door open and Sam came rushing to greet both of us as long-lost friends. Ronnie was taking his sleeping-bag out of his Land-rover.

I drove home. My mind was not on the road as it should have been and I nearly hit the back of an artic before I pulled myself together. Janet had supper waiting for me. She took one look and then asked whether the Sergeant was coming on Sunday evening. I said that he was.

'About time I got a look at him,' she said.

NINE

A flying visit to Wallace delayed me in the morning. Ronnie had already left for work when I arrived at the club.

The unguarded interval had been no more than an hour, but there had been time enough for the place to seem overrun with children from the timeshare flats. On closer study there were only five, but those five had between them the energy and malice of a whole swarm of tenement kids. No serious damage had been done as yet, but two of the eldest were ready to defy my attempts to get rid of them. And they could run faster than I could.

The usually mild Sam sensed my anger and his hackles rose. If he bit a child, for however valid a reason, he might be put down. I left him shut in the jeep.

Dad keeps a catapult in the jeep, for lofting decoy pigeons and knocking off the occasional rabbit which has scraped a secure little bunker under the gorse and dares the dog to come and get it. I fetched it out, filled my pockets with pebbles and set to work. I had never before been cursed so foully nor in such posh accents, but they scooted away towards the water, took off in three canoes which had been pulled in to a tree-lined inlet in the bank of the reservoir and paddled back towards the Country Club.

After that, I had little to do but to wait for Harry Noble to keep his appointment – if word had reached him that the club was still functioning. I loafed in the shade and decided that enough sunshine was enough. I would hate to live in California. A day of good, Scottish

120

drizzle would be a welcome change when it came, which would be soon enough.

Harry had been something senior and technical in the oil industry until a falling derrick mashed his left shoulder. Invalided out with a pension and a lump sum, he had gone into business for himself as a consultant and by all accounts was doing well. He seemed to have all that a man could wish for – money and the freedom to choose his own working hours. That he chose to spend his money and much of his leisure at the one sport which his accident had made difficult for him was his own affair. Men climb mountains, not because they're there but because they're difficult.

He arrived in the early afternoon in a light blue Audi; a tall man and broad almost to the point of being stout, with a cheerful face, cropped fair hair and smiling blue eyes. He was light on his feet and always gave the impression of being as fit as a fiddle – except that he could not lift his left elbow more than a few inches from his waist, a disability which he had learned a thousand tricks to conceal.

He greeted me as if I were his long-lost daughter, putting his right arm round my waist and swinging me off my feet. I accepted the familiarity as being from one consultant to another. 'Did Keith get away all right?' he asked.

'I presume so,' I said. 'I haven't heard from them yet, but if they'd missed the ship they'd have been home again by now.'

'That figures. Peter Hay phoned to say that Herbie Tullos was dead but that you'd be carrying the ball until they found somebody else. He also said that you'd be continuing to give coaching.'

'I am. But I don't know much about coaching a man who shoots one-handed.'

'Nobody does. At least you can tell me where I'm missing. That's all that Herb Tullos ever did for me.'

'All right,' I said. 'If I can't do more than that, I won't charge you a fee for the lesson.'

'It's a pleasure doing business with you.'

'The pleasure's mutual. Show me your membership card.'

He laughed and showed me his card. 'The season will be on us soon,' he said as we descended to the Sporting layout, 'and I've joined a small pheasant syndicate. It's probably money down the drain, but I'm damned if I'm going to give up my pleasures just because some damn fool can't keep his ironmongery upright. I look to you to see that I get my money's-worth and don't let the others down. I get by all right on most low birds, but high crossers tend to keep on going.'

Sam came along with us. I opened up the tower and switched on the trap. Harry's gun was a nice little twenty-bore with a full pistol grip. He handled it well but when I started sending the clays over he hit only one of the first four. He missed once in front and twice underneath.

'Let's get your feet right for a start,' I said. 'Point your left foot where you intend to take the bird and take your weight on the right foot . . . That looks better. Try again.'

He hit two of the next four. 'You're trying to swing through,' I said, 'but your right hand's trying to do too many jobs; it doesn't have anything to spare for timing a trigger-pull. And sometimes you let your hand sag slightly with effort.' I stopped and thought about it. 'This isn't the advice I'd give any other shooter,' I said, 'but your problems aren't their problems. Well, at least you can't use your left hand to check your swing. Do you find the gun heavy?'

He had to think about it. 'Not heavy. Unwieldy, perhaps.'

'Then it might help if I add a little weight to the butt to improve the balance. Meanwhile, try using a maintained lead. Imagine another clay about two feet in front of the real one, aim at it, swing with it and fire without checking.'

He broke three in a row and then missed again. 'You were under,' I told him. 'Is your wrist getting tired?'

'A little.'

'It won't, in the field. Don't let your hand drop. Swing a straight line, not a rainbow.'

He was powdering four out of five by the time his cartridges ran short. 'You've earned a fee,' he said. 'That's the first time I've had coaching which went beyond "Next time hit the damned thing." You'll make some cripple a wonderful wife.'

I tried to look demure, modelling my expression on that of Mrs Hickson. 'Are you by any chance paying me the highest compliment a man can pay to any woman?' I asked.

He grinned at me. 'No, I'm bloody well not,' he said. 'When I take a wife, she'll be a rotten shot. I still have my pride. I'll square up with you before I go.'

'Let me try the weight of your gun.' I took it from him and tried mounting and swinging it one-handed. I lacked his muscles, but that lack helped me to sense the stresses on his right hand. 'Do you trust me?' I asked him. 'If you leave the gun with me for a couple of days, I think I could help you.'

'You've been right so far,' he said.

I noticed that he was using Eleys. I was standing over the place where I had found the mark of the shooting-stick.

'You were up here on Monday evening, weren't you?' I said. As soon as the words were out, I remembered the Sergeant's admonition to be careful.

But he only nodded. By common consent we moved to one of the seats. I took off my Skeet vest and spread it to keep my skirt clean.

'What did happen to Herb Tullos?' he asked. 'Some sort of accident with a trap, I gathered. Easily done, I suppose.'

'Haven't the police spoken to you?'

'I've been on an oil-rig since Tuesday morning, arguing about safety standards. What's more, I'm due to fly out to another rig in . . .' he glanced down at a large wrist-watch which was almost obscured by sub-dials and adjustable

123

rings '. . . in three hours' time. It's only a quickie. If I can approve the work I'll be back in time for tomorrow's competition. So don't start any work on my gun that you can't finish by tomorrow.'

'And if you can't approve the work on the rig?'

'Days. Or indefinitely. Who knows?'

What would my Sergeant want me to do? 'They may be trying to reach you.' I said. 'But they don't know that you were here on Monday. Perhaps you'd better tell me about it and I'll pass it on. And they're eliminating cartridges. I'll keep a few of yours for them.'

'Herb wasn't shot, was he?'

'No. It looked as if he'd been caught across the head by a trap-arm, but they want to be sure. They're identifying the last few visitors by the cartridges they left behind them.'

Harry thought it over. 'That seems reasonable,' he said at last. 'You can tell them that I only have the one gun and I was using the same batch of cartridges.

'I had an hour or two to spare, so I took a chance and came up on Monday evening, rather late. Eightish, perhaps. The club's closed on Mondays in theory, but if Herb was free he never minded you getting a bit of practice, provided that you slipped him the occasional fiver or a bottle at Christmas. I think that he was glad to have company. It must be lonely up here, outside of working hours.

'He was his usual cheerless and unhelpful self. I had another go at the same birds we've been working on today and he sat behind me and told me that I was missing them, which I could see for myself.'

'Was anybody else here?' I asked.

'Not a soul while I was here. If it's any help, I passed another car as I was leaving. That was around ten o'clock. It was slowing down, so I think the driver intended to turn in here.'

'Light-coloured, was it?'

'I think so. Grey or maybe blue. The sun was almost down and I'd been dazzled coming out of the gates. And, anyway, I'd no reason to notice it particularly.'

There would be a hundred things that the Sergeant would want to know, but I could think of only one or two more questions. 'Was Mr Tullos sitting on that folding stool of his?'

'You ask the damnedest questions,' Harry said, 'but I'll pay you the compliment of assuming that you have a reason for them. As a matter of fact, no. Herb had been doing a bit of gardening in that bed on the clubhouse side of the Skeet layouts when I showed up. I had cartridges and the right money to pay for my clays and his time, so there was no reason for either of us to go into the clubhouse. While I was getting my gun out of the car he asked if he could borrow my shooting-stick, and he used that.'

So much for the shooting-stick! 'He didn't shoot with you?' I asked.

'No. He said that he could only dig for a few minutes at a time before his back played him up. He was going to give himself some practice at Ball-trap, later. His gun was out on the grass beside him while he was gardening, laid out on his Skeet vest with a box of cartridges.'

The background to Mr Tullos's death was becoming clearer. My Sergeant would be pleased with me. I decided to see if I couldn't make his day. 'You wouldn't happen to know whether he ate a chocolate bar?'

Harry blinked at me. 'You must be psychic,' he said. 'I was hungry when I arrived, so I took out a bar of chocolate. I offered him a piece. He enjoyed it so much that he was almost dribbling, so I took another bar out of my stock for him. I always carry a few in the car.'

'And that would have been what time?'

Harry shrugged. 'Best guess, eight-twenty.'

Harry departed, en route for his oil-rig. I locked his gun away and then took a walk round, assuring myself that all was ready for the weekend's rush of activity.

There was a light breeze now to mitigate the heat of the day and sails were out on the water. I decided that sunshine was tolerable after all. Even if we had the Greenhouse Effect and all those little aerosols to thank for it, an occasional warm summer would make it almost worthwhile.

The central fact of Herbert Tullos's death was surrounded, I told myself, by bits and pieces of discombobulated fragmentism. Possibly the police, by patient teamwork, were fitting piece to piece and making a whole. Or possibly not. Unless they had found something illuminating in the way of contact traces or other mute evidence, it seemed to me that they were working from insufficient data. The only witnesses on land had been too engrossed in adultery to spare a glance for anything so unromantic as a murder. But had the cops asked whoever had charge of the dinghies whether anyone had been out sailing, late on Monday evening?

I would ask my Sergeant. He wouldn't tell me, but I would ask him anyway. If he ever showed his face again. Perhaps I had frightened him off and some female officer, built like a Russian weightlifter, would take his place.

Keeping an occasional eye cocked in the direction of the clubhouse I had wandered towards the bright water, leaving the orderly paths and lawns of the club for an uneven terrain of weeds, wild flowers, stands of birch and alder and sudden patches of marshy land. A mallard left her nest in a hurry, circling until I turned away. A weasel abandoned the carcass of a carrion crow and undulated into cover.

My wandering had brought me closer to the trees sheltering the small inlet. A movement caught my eye. If my mind had not still been toying with the idea of water-borne witnesses, I would probably have ignored it. I walked casually in that direction, pretending great interest in the further hills. If one of those kids had returned, a clip round the ear would be followed by some stern questions.

There was another canoe in the inlet. The boy who was lying comfortably in a well-used nest, between two trees and sheltered by the underbrush, was unembarrassed. A pair of binoculars lay by his hand. He was older than the kids I had chased away, but rather young for an assassin – I put him at fifteen, give or take a year – and anyway I recognised the rifle at his side as a moderately expensive airgun. He was tall, built on the lines of a pipe-cleaner although I thought that once he had filled out he would be sturdy. He had a likeable, sensible face and his brown hair, in need of a trim, had a natural curl which I envied.

'Birdwatching?' I asked.

'In a sense,' he said guardedly.

'What sense?'

'I like to watch the clay pigeon shooting. You call them birds, don't you?' His accent was faintly Scottish but undoubtedly better than mine.

'True.' I could have pointed out that he was committing an offence by having an uncovered air weapon in a public place. On the other hand, perhaps his only error was in not having paid for a day membership of the club on whose land he was. I was unsure of the law.

'Joe – the man who looks after the boats at the Country Club – lets me take out a canoe whenever I want if I help him to look after the dinghies when he's busy. I was watching you yesterday evening,' he said. 'You're quite good.'

'Thanks.' I looked towards the Skeet layouts. 'But how would you know? There's a low safety banking at the top of the rise. When you're shooting, you can't even see the water, let alone the nearer shore. So you couldn't possibly see who was shooting from here.'

He sighed. The need to explain himself to nosy adults was getting to be too much. 'I could tell which shots were yours. Your gun sounds different from most of the others. What were you using? A four-ten?'

127

'Twenty-bore. If you want to spectate,' I said, 'why don't you come up to the club?'

'I'm not allowed near the place. The parents think it's dangerous. I'm saving up for my own gun and I'll soon be old enough to suit myself.'

'If you think it's safer down here, you're out of your mind,' I told him.

He grinned at me. 'You get a little spent shot pattering down now and again. It's nothing to signify.'

That was probably true. He was outside normal range of the small shot allowed for clay pigeons, and none of the members was likely to use a gun or cartridge faulty enough to cause balling of the shot.

Most of the time, he was meeting my eyes frankly. In between, he was getting a good look at my legs from his low viewpoint. I stepped back a pace. That privilege was reserved for Sergeant Fellowes. I decided that this stripling quite fancied me but was too young and uncertain to do anything about it.

'Were you here on Monday evening?' I asked.

'When that man was killed? No.' He sounded disappointed. 'I know somebody who might have been,' he added.

'A lady and a gentleman?' I asked, although I doubted whether either description really applied.

'You know? No, I wasn't thinking of them,' he said slowly.

'Who, then?'

'I don't think I should tell you that. I could see if he'll come and talk to you.'

'I'd be grateful.'

He looked at me speculatively. For a moment, unjustly, I thought he was going to suggest that the pleasure of my little pink body might be a satisfying way to express my gratitude. But apparently his development had not yet reached that stage. 'I bet I could hit a clay pigeon with my airgun,' he said.

128

That sounded like *folie de grandeur* to me, but I went along with him. 'I bet you couldn't,' I said.

'I can hit birds flying,' he said.

I looked at him sternly. 'You do realise that everything's out of season?'

'Carrion crows aren't.'

Nobody who killed carrion crows could be all bad. 'Get him to come and talk to me,' I said, 'and I'll put some easy clays over your head, and if you can hit even one of them with your airgun I'll give you some tuition with a proper shotgun. For free. And tell your parents that you can come and spectate from the clubhouse windows, any time.'

He launched the canoe and paddled away in the direction of the Country Club. He turned round once to give me a cheerful wave and nearly overbalanced the thing. He was out of sight before I remembered that I had not asked his name.

By the time the Sergeant showed up, I was being run off my feet.

The weekend rush did not usually start until Friday evening, but that day it built up through the afternoon as those who could start the weekend early came to sharpen up for the competitions of the next two days. Along with the well-heeled self-employed came several whom I knew to be unemployed or on sick-leave. It was only human to wonder where they had found the money that they were uncomplainingly handing over to me.

I began to wish that I had been nicer to the late Mr Tullos. He had had a right to be scratchy. Even with both legs in working order, I was hard pushed. Until help arrived, I found that I was expected to be cook and barmaid, cashier, trapper and scorer, safety officer, trap-loader, umpire and referee. By refusing to unlock several of the trap-houses, I managed to keep separate groups shooting the disciplines at which they wanted to

129

practice while keeping them out of each other's lines of fire and areas where they might be hit by falling clays. After that I retired to the clubhouse, breathing deeply and telling myself not to panic.

The Sergeant turned up before things got quite out of hand. He listened to my news, nodded, and took over duty behind the bar. This I put down to his kind and thoughtful nature, until I realised that while taking entries he was able to jot down the names and addresses of all day-members.

I was looking around, trying to anticipate the next crisis, when I was accosted suddenly by a well-dressed middle-aged man with an authoritative manner and a moustache to match. I had a faint recollection of having seen him before, performing competently at English Sporting. I thought at first that he was another member, about to complain that he wanted to shoot at some stand from which he would endanger everybody else, until I recognised him as Hugh Glencorse, the Club Secretary.

'You seem to have things in hand,' he said briskly. 'Plenty of volunteers? Well done! I've brought you out the week's catering supplies.'

A stripling appeared from nowhere to help us carry the cartons in from Mr Glencorse's large estate car. When the freezer and bar stocks were replenished, I prepared to dash outside to cope with whatever emergency was next to arise.

'You've earned a rest,' Mr Glencorse said. 'Sit down and have a cup of coffee with me. Or would you like a proper drink? One thing certain is that somebody will fetch you if you're needed.'

I was glad to subside at one of the few unoccupied tables. I felt that my legs were trailing along the ground behind me, and Sam had insisted on being put back in the jeep. It takes a lot of mileage to tire a Labrador. 'Thank you,' I said. 'A shandy, please, and a long sit-down.'

He came back with my shandy and a low alcohol lager

for himself. The Sergeant, still behind the bar, must have recognised him because no money passed.

'Now,' he said. 'What problems?'

'Nothing very special,' I told him. 'I sent one man to sit in his car for an hour, for unsafe gun-handling, and told him that if it happened once more he'd be sent home. He told me that I didn't have the authority.'

Mr Glencorse drew himself up. 'Who was it?' he asked. 'I'll have the committee speak to him.'

'No need. I was quite prepared to pull the main fuse and shut the place down but the members who'd complained ganged up on him.'

'Well done. What else?'

'Nothing very much. Three men were sharing a hip-flask. I thought it would soon be empty, but I heard one of them say something about the Widow's Cruse. So I told them that it was probably filling up with spit as fast as they emptied it. They seemed to lose interest in it after that.'

He nodded in satisfaction. 'Everything under control, then?'

'More or less. There's one problem. I have thirty or more members and guests out there practising Skeet, DTL and English Sporting. I can't keep a check on all of them. I'm jolly sure that some of them are paying for twenty birds and shooting at fifty or more.'

'We needn't worry too much. Keep a check on one or two of them and catch them out. Tell them you're reporting them to the committee. That usually provokes a temporary resurgence of honesty in the others.' He paused and raised an eyebrow at me. 'You're enjoying yourself?'

'It's a novelty,' I said, 'and sort of fun.'

'If we got somebody to stay in the house and be around in the mornings – I'm thinking of one of the members who's a chef and lives alone in digs – would you take it on permanently? Feedback says that you're doing well and the members like you.'

That came as a bombshell. If I had given any thought

to a permanent career it had been as a general helper to Dad. 'I don't know,' I said. 'I'll have to think about it.'

'Of course you will. I've no right to spring it on you like this. But while you think about it, will you at least help us out for a minimum of six weeks? Sir Peter has Sam Pollinder in mind and he'd do at a pinch, but he's got himself committed to marking exam papers before he can retire and then he wants a holiday. Personally, I don't think his health's up to it.'

'I think I could promise you six weeks.'

He sipped his lager and looked at me over the rim of the glass. 'What do you think about the idea of the club being bought out by the neighbours?'

The apparent change of subject made me stare. 'I'd hate that,' I said.

He nodded satisfaction. 'You see those two men at the bar?'

I looked. There were several men at the bar, but only two who seemed to be together. 'The ones with the dog?'

'Yes. They were only elected last week. But I happened to bump into one of them on Monday evening at the theatre. He seemed keen to sell. I now think that they may have been put up to it by the management at the Leisure Centre. Two members suddenly voting the wrong way might swing it. What I'd like you to tell me is that you'll bridge the gap for six weeks in exchange for being given a life-membership.'

I thought for a few moments and then it made sense. 'You're padding the membership to avoid the takeover. And it'll cost you almost nothing, because Dad has a family membership anyway. Right?'

'You've got it.'

'But you're giving me a financial incentive to vote for a sell-out.'

He had a surprisingly warm smile. 'We trust you,' he said.

'All right. I'll help you out for at least six weeks in exchange for a life-membership.'

132

He smiled again. 'I think that we can meet your terms. We have a committee meeting this evening. I'll put it to them.'

Somebody came panting up from the lower level to say that the shooters wanted the Bolting Rabbit trap-house unlocked. And one of the DTL traps had run dry. And somebody was shooting a third round of Skeet, very slowly, and wouldn't make way for those who were waiting. And the practice at the Sporting layout had grown into an informal competition and there was a dispute about the rules.

I hurried outside and began to dispense a sort of palmtree justice.

Mr Glencorse's mention of volunteers had stirred up some sediment in my mind. I had been vaguely aware of a few late teenagers who were bustling about and making themselves generally useful as trappers and scorers and golfers. They seemed to know the jargon and the routine. Although I did not recall any of their faces and I had assumed that they were Mr Tullos's regulars. I sent one of them for more cartons of standard clays, unlocked the Rabbit trap-house, settled several arguments and then watched. I saw one of the young fellows pick up a brace of spent cartridges, scribble something on them with a felt-tip pen and drop them into his pocket. He seemed to be muttering to himself, but when I crept up on him I found that he was dictating a pungent but recognisable description of the cartridges' owner into his own button-hole. Somewhere beneath the jeans and loose golf-jacket was a midget, portable tape-recorder.

I climbed back up to the clubhouse and accosted the Sergeant behind the bar. 'Those beardless youths,' I said. 'The ones who are doing all the work. Are they policemen? I must be getting old.'

He gave me his special grin. 'Police cadets,' he said.

Fair enough. I found myself wondering whether we couldn't spin the mystery out for another six weeks.

Later, I had to unlock the house so that the committee could meet in the sitting-room. They duly elected me a life-member. Some of them even stayed on to help clear up.

I arrived home earlier than I had expected and then stayed up half the night altering Harry's gun.

TEN

In summer, Saturday was usually the busiest day at the Pentland Gun Club. (During the winter, with game and wildfowl shooting in full swing and the evenings dark, the peak of activity shifted to Sunday.) I had hopes that the day would prove less hectic than usual, the serious competitors being away striving for gold or glory and only the potterers present for a couple of friendly and informal competitions.

I seemed to be running out of clothes that were cool and comfortable and yet not too unflattering. The needs of my new occupation fell somewhere between my less disreputable clothes, which had been bought with an eye to jaunts around the Edinburgh discos, and the sort of rags in which I might have gone ratting or rabbiting or heather-burning with Ronnie. Mum, on the other hand, had bought new clothes for her holiday. If she had been at home, she would certainly have lent me something, I told myself. I borrowed a good white blouse and a pair of cream slacks which she had been saving against the day when dieting or a miracle might enable her to wear them again. Even Mum would have admitted that they looked better on me.

Giving Harry's gun a last touch-up delayed me. I was late, but Uncle Ronnie, on a day off, had waited for me. I had intended to coax him into helping me fill the magazines of all the traps and generally ready the place for business. But he was arrayed in his best suit, the one which makes him look like a bookmaker on a losing streak, so I guessed that

he was set for a weekend of lechery and booze. His Land-
rover started off, bouncing suggestively over the bumps
in the gravel as though it had caught his mood, leaving
Sam to stare disgustedly after it. He knew that he would
usually get more sport with Ronnie than with me. There
was no sign of the Sergeant, who was attending another
briefing.

I was not alone for long. I had lugged some cartons
of clays to the top of the steps, to await the arrival of the
first customer who could be persuaded to distribute the
heavy boxes for me, when I felt eyes on me and realised
that the boy from yesterday was watching me shyly from
the lower level.

'Come on up,' I said. 'You can give me a hand.'

He climbed the steps, carrying his airgun under one
arm, and stooped to give Sam a quick pat.

'The first and unbreakable rule,' I said, 'is that guns
are carried open and empty at all times. And I don't know
your name.'

He grinned and broke open his airgun. 'I'm Paul
Fettercairn,' he said. 'I've got something for you.'

I returned his grin. I liked the boy. And, besides, he
could be useful. 'A strong back, I hope. The second
rule is that guns are never left lying around. We've never
had a theft, but there's no point in putting temptation in
somebody's way.'

We locked the airgun in the jeep and then each picked up
a box of the special clays for the Bolting Rabbit. He turned
out to be stronger than he looked. 'Don't drop it,' I said.
'They're supposed to break in the air, not to trickle out of
the box as a fine powder. Now, what have you found out?'

'There's a boy,' he said. 'He doesn't want to be named,
but he often takes a canoe out late. He came down this
way on Monday evening. He was early, so he'd nothing
to do but look around.'

Three paces later, the significance struck me. 'Early
for what?' I asked. 'Was he meeting somebody?'

'Sort of, but not exactly. He's a bit of a creep.'

Paul was being evasive. One possible explanation occurred to me. 'He's a Peeping Tom, is he?'

'Nothing like that,' Paul said hastily. 'He stays down where you saw me yesterday. He just feels he has to know. It's probably one of those things which somebody else could never understand. If it was me, I'd pretend it wasn't happening. But I suppose I'm good at burying my head in the sand. I never look at exam results until I have to.'

That I could understand. 'Nor did I.'

We arrived at the Bolting Rabbit trap-house. He watched as I filled the magazine and stowed the rest of the clays in a corner. It seemed to me that we were talking about the son either of Mrs Hickson or of her lover.

'What did he see?' I asked as we walked back.

'Somebody was shooting, up on top where the Skeet is. He couldn't see anything much because of the hump, but, from what he said, whoever it was was pretty good and didn't miss much. Then several minutes passed with nothing happening except that he could hear voices. Then a man came down the steps.'

'Was he carrying a gun?'

'No.'

We had reached the steps ourselves. Paul stopped half-way up and pulled a piece of paper out of his back pocket. 'I drew a rough map,' he said. 'The man looked around for a bit and then went and picked something up from here and here.' Paul touched some mysterious symbols on his sketch-map. 'Then he says that the man put down whatever he'd picked up about here.'

The sketch-map was clear and remarkably accurate, and it was not difficult to guess that the mysterious man had been moving unbroken clays from where they had been thrown by the Skeet traps to the position in which I had pointed them out to the Sergeant. If he had missed four, he couldn't be so very good. On the other hand, he could have tried out the acoustic release before starting to shoot.

But the acoustic release had ended up in the Ball-trap trap-house. Perhaps it had been there all the time.

'Go on,' I said.

'There isn't much more. He was still down at the bottom level when he heard a laugh. People were coming.'

Beatrice Hickson had a laugh that would scare pigeon off a field of oilseed rape, upwind. 'What did he do?' I asked.

'He hurried back and went up the steps, almost running. And that was all my friend saw because he wasn't looking this way after that. Does it help?' Paul asked anxiously.

'What was the man like?'

'It was a long way off. All he could say was that the man was wearing dark trousers, a white shirt and one of those greenish waistcoats that they mostly wear. And he had a blue cap on, sort of like a baseball cap.'

'That's what about ninety per cent of them wear,' I said.

'Don't blame me if he's one of the great majority,' Paul said seriously. 'He had a bit of a tummy on him, if that's any help. His hands were dark. Either he was wearing gloves or he'd been groping in mud. Oh, and there was a dog stuck to his heal like glue. A black dog like yours.'

I glanced down. I had quite forgotten that Sam was following at my heel, waiting for something interesting to happen. 'Has he told the police?'

'Yes, days ago. The boatman put them onto him. He told them about the man, not about the other people. But they seemed to know.'

So the Sergeant had known a lot more than he had told me. Well, damn him!

'Come and fetch your airgun,' I said. 'We can finish carting the clays around later. Somebody may even turn up to help.'

I gave him some slowish, overhead clays from the tower. I heard his pellet connect with the fourth one although it didn't break – modern clay pigeons are made stronger than the older ones, to withstand the stress of the higher-speed traps. The boy was going to be good, some day.

'Fair enough,' I said. 'you'll get your lessons.'

'When?'

'When I have some free time,' I said. 'Keep in touch.'

The Sergeant turned up a few minutes later with his police cadets. They helped us to distribute the rest of the clays. I thanked the lads warmly, but I was rather cold with the Sergeant.

The first shooters to arrive did so in a fawn Mercedes. They were the two stout men whom Mr Glencorse, the Club Secretary, had pointed out at the bar.

'You're members?' I was duty bound to ask the question even though I thought that I knew the answer.

'Certainly,' said the younger of the two. 'Are you?'

It seemed a needlessly offensive question to ask of a steward. I was glad to retort that I was a life-member, although it had only been true for about eighteen hours.

They produced their membership cards as though they were insulted to have been asked for them. Douglas Pender was the one in his forties, a tubby yet angular man with an arrogant glare. At some time his nose had been broken, giving him the look of a retired bruiser. Alistair Wyman was rather older but seemed to spark with nervous energy. Their cards gave the address for each as c/o Wyman and Pender, Jewellers, with an address in the Royal Mile, Edinburgh.

They paid for a round of Skeet as well as for the afternoon's Sporting competition, bought a box of cartridges and went off to shoot.

Oliver Gray arrived alone. I had picked out a slightly used Fabarm Multichoke as being suited to both his build and his sport. He looked at it without any great enthusiasm. 'I never liked over-unders much,' he said.

'You don't have a master-eye problem?' I asked him.

An over-under presents a broader picture to the non-aiming eye.

'Not that I've ever noticed. If anything, my left eye's the weaker.'

'Give it a fair trial, then. You'll find that the extra weight mops up the recoil.' I showed him how to select and fit the five chokes. 'The law says that you have to buy it or return it by tonight,' I finished. 'For today, it's all yours.'

I took him down to one of the stands at the tower to get some practice, with young Paul to press the buttons for him, and left them to get on with it.

Cars were trickling in now and I was accosted by a group of aspiring shooters wanting to know what competition I had arranged for them and when it would start and how much was the entry – all of it information which they could have gleaned from the notice-board. Three tough-looking young men with beards and black leathers arrived on motorbikes with cased shotguns on the panniers. They turned out to be the politest and best-behaved of all the shooters present.

Harry Noble turned up, looking as bright as a silver trophy although he must have been working or travelling half the night. I fetched his twenty-bore from the car. He looked startled at the sight of it.

'Don't howl 'til you're hurt,' I told him. 'You were tilting your barrels to the left because your shoulder-pocket, which the butt's supposed to settle into, isn't up and down but runs from your neck to your armpit. So I've given you an adjustable butt-pad and twisted it anti-clockwise. That should find your shoulder-pocket every time without giving your right hand yet another job to do. And I've included a shim of lead to bring the balance further back.'

'But it looks peculiar,' he said.

'Does that matter, if it works for you?'

'Not a bit.'

'Go and try it,' I told him. 'We can argue after we know what we're arguing about.'

The Sergeant, who, I was pleased to see, was either ignoring my coolness or had failed to notice it, was checking memberships, taking entries, distributing score-cards and selling cartridges as if born to it. I thanked him with a little more warmth. It was hardly his fault that he was a bad communicator.

Members and visitors were gathering in penny numbers, changing shoes or jackets, unbagging guns, counting cartridges, sipping coffee or calling for last-minute snacks before going into battle. The carpark was still only half full. With the serious competitors and their close friends drawn away to more important and rewarding competitions, I was relieved to see that I knew most of the faces and that no dedicated cash-chasers were among them. Tradition dictated that half the entry fees were returned as prize money, and small numbers would mean modest prizes and less incentive for arguments.

Outside the door, I had time for a few deep breaths. Mr Pender and Mr Wyman were coming back from the Skeet layouts, the black Labrador at heel. The men were squabbling about something.

'. . . not my fault you can't shoot Skeet,' Mr Pender was saying.

'It's your fault I don't have the right gun with me,' Mr Wyman retorted. 'This one's all right for Sporting, but at Skeet it's like trying to swat midges with a rolling pin.'

He stumped angrily off towards his car. Douglas Pender watched him go and then, turning away, realised that I was standing nearby.

'Not everybody can lose gracefully,' he said. 'You told us that you're a life-member? I find that hard to believe.'

'It's true, all the same,' I told him. 'You're welcome to check with the Secretary.'

He grunted but decided to take my word for it, for the moment. 'I'm going to demand an extraordinary general meeting to discuss this offer from the Leisure Complex. How do you stand?'

'I'm not in favour.'

He produced his ready scowl and then wiped it away with a visible effort. I remembered Mr Glencorse's suspicion that he and his partner had been sponsored by the unpleasant Mr McGruer. 'It's not to everybody's taste,' he said, 'but there could be a substantial dividend for each member and enough left over to set up again elsewhere.' His neutral accent was an almost perfect imitation of a professional man but it had the bluntness which usually comes from hard beginnings.

'It's not easy to get planning permission for a noisy activity,' I said. 'There are always too many objectors. Usually, if you get it at all, it's on a year-by-year basis. That wouldn't encourage the club to re-invest in good facilities.'

He narrowed his eyes. 'There could be something extra in it for yourself,' he suggested.

'Not interested,' I said. 'And you can tell your friend Mr McGruer.'

'Never met the man. I'm looking on it as I would any other investment.'

'Did you join the club as an investment?' I asked him.

He glared at me again and then produced a bark of laughter which was more akin to a snarl. 'I joined because I heard that it was the best value for money. But only a born fool passes up the chance of an easy profit. You think about that, my girl.'

He turned away from me. His Labrador, sensing discord, rumbled deeply at Sam who looked away, disdaining to notice such behaviour. I was pleased to see a large plaster covering a lump on the back of Mr Pender's neck. He put up a hand to it and then glanced round and met my eye. It seemed to embarrass him. 'Getting a bit old for adolescent acne,' he said. 'But I can still shoot.'

There was no profit in being at war with a member. 'I'm sure you can,' I said. 'How did you do on the Skeet?'

'Twenty-three.'

'That's not bad,' I said. He nodded and walked stiffly away without another word. Any more lip from him, I thought, and I would take hold of that lump and squeeze.

Sir Peter Hay was climbing stiffly out of his Land-rover and groping in the back for his leather gun-case. I walked over to him.

'Afternoon, my dear,' he said. 'Looks like a small turnout. Ah well, all the more chance for the duffers among us. Are you giving us some birds I might be able to catch up with?'

'I'm giving you an easy start,' I said. 'It gets a bit more difficult later, but if you stay cool and keep your swing going you'll be all right.'

I was hesitating between thanking him again for my life-membership and repeating my conversation with Mr Pender, but I was distracted. Sir Peter had parked beside the fawn Mercedes and a movement behind the darkened glass caught my eye. Somebody – presumably Alistair Wyman – was sitting in the passenger seat and I had a nasty feeling that he might be readying himself for competition with a stiff drink. I was brought up in a household where the taking of drink was a matter of no account, except prior to driving or shooting. As far as I was concerned Mr Wyman could drink until his liver curled up and died – but not if he was going to use a gun in my vicinity.

I stepped forward and jerked the door open.

Mr Wyman looked up at me. He was holding a hypo-dermic syringe and he had rolled up a shirtsleeve. A neat case on the seat beside him held several rows of ampoules.

'What the hell?' I said. A drug addict would be worse than a drunk.

'Do you mind?' he said angrily. 'I happen to be diabetic. Three times a day or I collapse. Would it really bother you if I lived a little longer?'

It seemed to be my day for making enemies among my fellow members. 'I apologise,' I said. 'But I'm responsible for safety around here and if I see somebody "shooting up" – not in the gun sense – I have to look into it.'

'And have you finished?'

'Quite finished,' I said. 'Don't be long. I'll be starting the competition soon.' I closed the door gently and stepped back.

Sir Peter had remained in the background, but he had taken it all in. 'I wish we hadn't admitted those two,' he said quietly. 'They seemed all right. Best behaviour, I suppose. But I think they're going to be trouble.'

Four men had opted to go and have a private battle at Down the Line. And I had decided not to shoot, having more than enough on my plate already. So our fifty-bird Sporting was down to a mere dozen entrants.

Top-level competitions are usually conducted in comparative silence as the competitors study the birds and build up their concentration. Less formal shoots are more often occasions for chaff and banter. But for some reason that Saturday's competition started off in an atmosphere of bickering which steadily worsened. Douglas Pender was largely to blame. He had his knife into me from the start, and he and his partner seemed to have developed a dislike of Oliver Gray and Rambo Torrance which was reciprocated. The banter still flew. It was meant to seem light but it had a cutting edge.

The committee had left me a free hand in arranging the competition and, to avoid giving an extra advantage to the wealthier shooters, I had decreed that only one gun and one pair of chokes were to be used throughout – a rule more usual in FITASC than in English Sporting. The rule had been appended to the notice of the competition which I had pinned on the board, but Douglas Pender, still irritated by our earlier squabble, chose to believe that it was an act of discrimination against him personally. It took a sharp word from Sir Peter to quiet him.

The score-cards were shuffled to decide the order of

shooting and the first man stepped into the cage. I was starting them off with an easy pair of Driven Pheasants from the tower – birds approaching straight and slow overhead.

Oliver Gray, who was drawn to shoot second, touched my arm and tapped the action of the Fabarm. I lifted one muff of my ear-protectors. 'The recoil's much less,' he said. 'I'll give you that. But the bottom line is how often you hit the bird. And I'm not doing well.'

The Sergeant was scoring and young Paul had the trapper's job with the release control, so I was free to pay attention. 'I'll watch and tell you what you're doing wrong,' I promised.

Mr Gray took his place in the cage and missed both of his first pair. 'You lifted your head,' I said. 'You're still expecting a kick in the face. Keep your cheek down on the comb.' I spoke loudly because of the protectors over his ears.

He broke five of the remaining eight, not just chipping them but blowing them to dust. The other three he missed when he forgot and lifted his head again. Mr Pender objected strongly to an adversary being coached while shooting, although it must already have been obvious that Oliver Gray was not a serious contender.

There was nothing to be gained by argument. 'You're quite right,' I said. 'I'm sorry. He's never used that gun before. It won't happen again.'

'Right.' The firm of Wyman and Pender must have been making good money because he was nursing over his arm a Beretta with engraving which I recognised as being from the *Bottega* in Gardone, while his partner carried a very expensive Browning.

Tempers subsided as the contest developed into a pattern. Harry Noble and Sir Peter were not disgracing themselves but were resigned to bringing up the rear. The middle ruck, including Oliver Gray and the flirtatious Mrs Cowan, were relieved of any fear of turning in the lowest score and were having a cheerful contest among themselves.

Rambo Torrance, hitting a rare streak of form, was up with the leaders, fighting it out in grim determination with Alistair Wyman and a thin and sallow man from the Leisure Complex; but Douglas Pender, after a shaky start, controlled his temper and shot Bolting Rabbit and Springing Teal straight. He missed one pair on the Driven Grouse – a low, fast bird which flicked over the shooter's head – but he had done enough to bring himself into the lead.

The last stand was designed to separate the men from the boys – a settling bird from behind followed 'on report' by a fast, high crosser. As we reached the stand, I said to Oliver Gray, 'Take your time and don't hurry.'

Mr Pender, walking in front of us, stopped dead and swung round. 'You're doing it again,' he said.

His closed gun was pointing at my feet. 'Gun open and empty, please,' I said.

He was absolutely in the wrong and I was right to speak out and he knew it; but that only added to his fury. He dropped his barrels but I could see indignation building up inside him.

One of the members, a civil servant from the Scottish Office, black as coal but always charming, had been shooting a middling score with a Spanish game gun. He said quickly, 'I don't think that there can be any objection to somebody advising a friend during the walk between stands.'

Pender looked him up and down but decided against retorting with some racial slur.

'I could do with a friend like that,' one of the motorcyclists said.

'I'm sure she'd do as much for anybody else,' Oliver Gray said. He paused. 'Even for you,' he added grimly.

Douglas Pender's irregular nose flared brightly against the duller flush of his face. 'And just what makes her think that she's qualified to dish out advice?' he enquired through gritted teeth.

'She's qualified,' Harry Noble said, 'believe me.' One or two of the others murmured agreement.

Mr Pender looked around the faces. I was glad to see his scowl shared around the others for a change. 'You're all on her side because she's an attractive piece of skirt,' he said.

There was a moment of total silence. I saw Sergeant Fellowes move closer – perhaps to break it up if fists began to fly, or perhaps in the hopes of getting his own blow in.

'I rather think,' said the civil servant quietly, 'that in the circumstances we would give any steward our support.'

Douglas Pender hesitated again, unsure whether he could pick an insult out of the words.

'Are we going to shoot the last stand or not?' Sir Peter asked plaintively. 'I wish to know what I've won.' This remark, in Sir Peter's distinctive voice, and uttered by somebody who was already a dozen birds behind the leaders, shattered the tension. There was a general chuckle and the shoot resumed.

Oliver Gray broke eight out of ten. Douglas Pender, when his turn came, gave every appearance of having recovered his temper, but he was snatching hastily at the second bird of the doubles. He held second place but let the man from the timeshare flats through into a win. Harry Noble, gaining confidence in his altered gun, pulled away from Sir Peter and overtook Mrs Cowan.

According to custom, half the entry money went to the club and half was distributed as prizes. I had three tenners ready in my pocket. I presented a brace to the timeshare man, to a polite round of applause. When I handed the other to Douglas Pender, in an absolute silence, he pulled off his shooting gloves and almost snatched it.

'Perhaps you were well advised not to shoot,' he said.

I only nodded. 'Probably,' I said.

Others were less inclined to pass off the remark. 'Just what was that supposed to mean?' Rambo Torrance demanded.

Pender shrugged. 'She's ready enough with her mouth, but she doesn't seem to fancy shooting against the men.'

'Do you think you could beat her?' Torrance asked.

'I could shoot the pants off her.'

'That I would like to see,' said a voice.

I could feel a tremor of anger in the back of my neck but I forced myself to hide it. 'Well, you won't,' I said. 'My pants are not for shooting. Come on, now. It's time for food. Who's staying on to eat?'

Several hands were raised. I turned away towards the clubhouse.

'All mouth,' said Pender.

I turned back. 'What did you say?'

'I think you heard me.'

'Now, let's stay calm,' Alistair Wyman said smoothly. 'I'm sure Miss Calder has no objection to matching herself against you, Douglas.'

'You think so? How about fifty Skeet? Unless you'd rather teach her the much-needed lesson?'

'Thanks to your idiocy, I don't have my Skeet gun with me. You saw what a balls I made of trying to shoot Skeet with the wrong gun.'

'Leave it to me, then,' Pender said. 'I'll show her where she gets off.'

'Be fair,' Oliver Gray said. 'You've been shooting all afternoon. You've got your eye in. You should give her some advantage. Or don't you think you could "shoot the pants off her"?'

'All right,' Pender shouted. 'All bloody right. I won't shoot my optional birds. How about that?'

'Fifty quid says that she'll equal or beat you,' Harry Noble said.

'You're on,' Pender said.

'Just a moment,' I said. 'Don't I have any say in this?'

'My dear,' Sir Peter said gently, 'it doesn't look as if

you do.' It seemed to me that he was enjoying himself. He turned to Mr Pender. 'We'll eat first. Then I'll back Miss Calder to the tune of twenty-five.'

'I'll take it,' said Alistair Wyman.

'You'd better go home to your mother,' I told Paul. 'This may not be pretty.'

A strange new excitement was in the air. The atmosphere would have seemed fitting before a bullfight or a public hanging.

Most of those present, even those who had intended to rush away, elected to stay on and eat at the club. I was horrified. A private challenge was becoming a public contest.

The civil servant, who had an unpronounceable African surname but cheerfully answered to Reg, put the general attitude into a nutshell. 'I'm supposed to attend some dreary reception this evening,' he said. 'But I wouldn't miss this for the world. I shall plead the onset of beri-beri. I look forward to seeing you take that unpleasant gentleman down a peg or two. Those two have made themselves thoroughly disliked since they fooled the committee into admitting them.' He was a good-looking man, his looks accentuated rather than diminished by his colour, and his voice with its Oxbridge accent always made me feel as though my knees were about to develop a wobble.

'I may not be able to do it,' I pointed out.

'You can do it if you really want to,' he said. 'I saw you beat Angie Miller in the semi-final of the Skeet Championships.' He moved to the pay-phone to make his excuses.

The cadets had vanished, but the Sergeant helped me out by serving drinks while I ran a production-line through the microwave oven. I had brought food for Sam and I fed him first. It was not his fault that I was having unwanted responsibilities heaped on me.

The Sergeant picked up the last two meals and led

me to a vacant table. 'Calm down and take it easy,' he told me as we sat down. 'Relax. You've got to get the mood right.'

'On the contrary, I'd have to psych myself up,' I said. 'If I were going to do it. Which I'm not.'

'But you must. He needs taking down. If you back out now, he'll claim a victory and win his bets.'

'Anyway, what's it to you?'

'I've got twenty quid riding on you myself.'

'This is getting out of hand,' I said. Douglas Pender was good although I should have been a match for him. But Dad's twelve-bore Skeet gun, which I usually used for serious competition, was back at Briesland House and my twenty-bore, although lightly choked, threw tighter patterns than were ideal for Skeet.

Among the babel of chat, I could pick out some words. Betting was becoming complex; odds were quoted on victories by such-and-such a margin.

I got to my feet. 'Listen to me,' I said. Nobody paid any attention. 'Shut up the bloody lot of you!' There was instant silence. If I could have bottled it, it would have been worth a fortune to any mother. In any pub desecrated by a juke-box it would have sold better than the beer. 'I don't like needle-matches,' I said, 'but I'm prepared to shoot this one off if you'll stop all this betting. I don't want to feel responsible. And it's flat against CPSA rules.'

'Only for formal competitions,' Rambo said. 'And you backed yourself yesterday evening.'

'That was a pool. And modest side-bets are winked at. This is too organised.'

Several men tried to speak, but Sir Peter was one of them and the others gave way to the club's chairman. 'Nobody's making a book, Deborah,' he said. 'These are individual side-bets. And if we care to throw our money away . . .'

'It needn't bother you if you let them down,' Mr Pender finished for him.

After that I would not have cried off for the Four
Minute Warning. 'Well, if I have to shoot,' I said, 'I'm
damned if I'm doing the washing up as well.' I sat down.
'I'm squatting here until somebody else has done it.'

Rambo Torrance got to his feet. 'That seems fair enough,'
he said. He began to gather plates. Harry Noble went
behind the bar and ran hot water.

'This will conclude the day's shooting,' Sir Peter said.
'For non-shooters and non-drivers, the bar proper is open.'

There was a small cheer.

I fetched my twenty-bore from the jeep and two boxes
of Skeet cartridges from the store. I checked that I had a
few spare cartridges in the pocket of my Skeet vest – you
can need extra if 'no bird' is given for a faulty clay. My
muffs were still hanging round my neck. I was as ready
as I would be.

The washing-up was finished in remarkably short time.

We walked out together, followed by a small crowd
carrying their glasses. They were in festive mood but I
felt hollow.

Sam, still at my heel, rumbled to himself and I noticed
that the other Labrador was back with Douglas Pender.
'Your dog?' I asked, for something to break the cold
silence.

He thought it over and decided that he would not
demean himself if he replied to me. 'Alistair's,' he said.
'This bugger's a fanatic. He'll follow any man with a gun.'
He halted. I noticed for the first time that he had a belly
on him, but so did several of the others. 'Alistair, call your
stupid tyke away before he gets under my feet.'

Mr Wyman put his dog on a lead but Sam stayed with me.

We arrived at the Skeet layouts and I switched on the
traps. We agreed to go round together. We tossed a coin.
I won. I decided to shoot first at each station in the first
round and then to swap over.

Alistair Wyman had the release control. 'Hold everything. I want somebody neutral trapping,' I said. 'In English

Skeet, we're entitled to an immediate bird, not a delay of up to three seconds as in Olympic and ISU Skeet. I'm damned if I'll be bugged by variable delays.'

There were no offers from the bystanders. 'I don't think that there is anybody neutral,' Reg said.

'I could fetch the acoustic release,' I suggested.

'I'll give you immediate birds,' Mr Wyman said with exaggerated patience. His tone suggested that I was only putting off the evil moment when I would have to face harsh reality. 'Sir Peter can referee and he can call "no bird" if I delay the release. Fair enough?'

I nodded to Sir Peter. 'Fair enough,' I said. I stepped onto Station One and loaded. 'Are you ready?'

'Ready,' Wyman said.

'Pull!'

ELEVEN

Under normal competition conditions I would have expected to shoot clear rounds, perhaps missing a rare bird when my concentration flagged. (It is by those few, unpredictable misses that titles are won and lost.) Even with my twenty-bore, I would expect to average 24 out of 25.

This time, my concentration had gone for a walkabout. Too many other thoughts were competing for places in my mind; and I had been reminded by my poor performance in the 'mixed doubles' how missable a close, fast bird can be. I started badly, missing the first bird, with high house single on Station One – a disastrous way to start, because you only shoot well when you know in advance, without any shadow of doubt, that you will break every target.

I told myself to get it together . . . relax . . . hold the gun lightly. I placed it above the crossing point and then swung half-way towards the low house and half again. When my concentration felt right, I called for the low house bird, led it by a foot and saw it go to smoke.

Now for the double. I refocused my eyes by looking at the centre peg, renewed my concentration, called and broke both birds of the double. I felt my heart stop its pounding. I was back on the road.

Douglas Pender had shaken off his earlier temper. He set off as though he was due for a clear round, but dropped one of his pair on Station Four. As we came round the semicircle of stations the setting sun began to blaze into our eyes. Dazzled, I held on too long before shooting the first of the double on Station Seven and as a result missed both birds of the pair while he lost one of his singles.

We were half done and I was two birds down.

My 'optional bird' would be the first target which I had missed, the usually easy high house departing bird on Station One. I stood for a few seconds, breathing deeply and going over the drill in my mind, reminding myself to take time, plenty of time. Then I called and shattered the bird just above the crossing point.

Douglas Pender was not shooting his optional, so I was only one down at the turn. Not fatal – I had the advantage on another optional to come – but not good.

'Beer break,' called Sir Peter. 'And we'll give the competitors a moment to relax. Deborah, what will you take?'

My mouth was dry. I asked for a shandy. Several men trotted back to the clubhouse while general conversations broke out.

There was one seat set back from the semicircle of stations and by common consent this was left for Douglas Pender and myself. My knees were shaking with effort and I was glad to sit down. Douglas Pender subsided with a grunt at the other end of the bench. I felt it shake.

I decided that he was shooting too well. But, earlier, he had shown that his concentration failed when he was irritated. Well, it had worked with Mrs Hickson and it might work again. If nothing else, it might keep my adrenalin flowing. Nobody was close enough to overhear.

'I see that you use Express cartridges,' I said tentatively.

'What about it?' he asked the empty air.

'There were some used, late on Monday. Have the police been to see you yet?'

This time he looked round at me. 'Why would they?' he enquired.

I was tempted to go all the way, to accuse him of murder, but I had to restrain myself. If I overshot the facts he would know it and he would recover his balance.

'They've seen all the other members. I wonder why they left you out. Perhaps you're a suspect. Of course, they may be waiting for the result of the tests on cartridges.'

He glared at me for a few seconds before he asked, 'What the hell are you talking about?'

'Didn't you know?' I was beginning to enjoy myself. I decided to let the Sergeant keep his anonymity for a little longer. 'Those young lads who've been helping all afternoon, they're police cadets. They were collecting fired cartridges. The lab is matching firing-pin imprints against the cartridges which were at the top of the bin on Monday evening.'

He shrugged and looked away.

Sir Peter came back with my shandy but he wandered off to have a word with Harry Noble. Alistair Wyman arrived with a soft drink for Douglas Pender.

'She's been telling me about the police investigation,' Mr Pender said to him. 'You know what I mean? The steward who was killed here on Monday evening. They're looking at cartridges, trying to trace guns . . .'

Mr Wyman snorted. 'The little bitch is only trying to throw you,' he said. 'Don't let her cheap tricks get to you. Just stay cool and concentrate on showing her where she gets off.'

'That's right,' I said. I was becoming ever more certain that my needles had found a sensitive nerve. 'I wouldn't worry about it. The witness who saw somebody with a black dog at heel, moving clays around on Monday evening, will probably pick somebody else.'

'We were together on Monday evening,' Pender said hoarsely.

Something else came back to me but I could not remember exactly what had been said. Who had the Club Secretary been looking at as he spoke? 'That's not what Mr Glencorse told me,' was the best I could find to say.

'Don't listen to her,' Mr Wyman said urgently. 'Come away from there. How's your neck?'

Mr Pender got to his feet. 'Easier,' he said. 'I think it's burst.'

'Oh, what a shame,' I said to his retreating back.

I was only alone for a few seconds before Sir Peter called out, 'Are the competitors ready? Then let battle resume.'

At first, of the two of us, I think that I was more prey to nerves. I have never been able to shrug off angry words or clashes of personality. The layout, usually so familiar, seemed strange and the timing of my natural swing was ready to desert me. Douglas Pender, on the other hand, wore an agonised scowl but was keeping his concentration going with a visible effort. It showed in the stiffness of his neck and his audible breathing. I watched from behind him as he broke his four birds from Station One; and when I stepped forward to take his place the timing was clear in my mind again.

We had both found form. We each shot the ten birds from the first three stations straight. But then the tide turned. Perhaps his effort was too great to sustain. On Station Four he missed both birds of the double. I collected both of the singles, called for the double, took the high house bird first and early, swung on without waiting to see whether the clay had broken and took the other almost over the same spot. A faint mutter of approval told me that I had powdered them both. For the first time it came home to me that the watchers were almost universally on my side.

I had the lead, with the advantage of the optional bird to come. For no particular reason, my swing and my timing had recovered. This was my favourite sport which I had always found easy. My confidence peaked.

He missed only one of his six birds from Stations Five and Six, but I blew all six to dust. The mutter grew. Somebody clapped, instantly checked by Sir Peter.

We moved to Station Seven. This was the dangerous time, because relaxation can easily set in too soon. I told myself to concentrate, to ignore the sun, to watch the trap-house opening and go through the familiar motions.

Douglas Pender had concentrated too hard for too long. He was over the high house single and behind the low house bird.

'That's all,' Sir Peter said. 'No need to shoot the doubles.'

'What?' Douglas Pender was like a man waking from a bad dream.

'You're four down and two birds to shoot. Even if Miss Calder missed all her birds you can't win now.'

'I see.' He turned away, pushed his gun into Alistair Wyman's hands. 'Oh, well. It's only money.'

Alistair Wyman broke open the gun and withdrew a pair of cartridges. 'Of course it is,' he said cheerfully. (But, of course, it wasn't.) 'Open and empty, Miss Calder? You go and have a drink, Douglas. I'll settle up for you.'

Douglas Pender hobbled towards the clubhouse like a very old man.

People were shaking my hand. More than one man pushed money into it, saying that he had put a few pounds on for me. Somebody kissed me, but I was only beginning to emerge from my trance of concentration and I never noticed who it was. Somebody else had smuggled out the bottle of champagne which had been kept in reserve for the climax of the next charity shoot. Paper cups were filled and one was pushed at me. I took it, but I had no stomach for a general celebration. I wanted to be alone, or almost alone. I caught the Sergeant's eye and then slipped away, round to the back of the clubhouse to where I could sit at the top of the bank, getting grass stains on Mum's slacks and looking over the Sporting layout.

The Sergeant joined me a few minutes later, dropping down beside me. 'Oliver Gray left this for you.'

'Thanks.' I glanced at the cheque to be sure that he had, as bidden, written the number of his shotgun certificate on the back before putting it into a pocket of my Skeet vest.

We sat in silence for a while, winding down. The Sergeant smiled suddenly. 'You did it,' he said. 'I thought for a while that you were going to let me down.'

'I'm not exactly proud of the way I did it,' I said.

'What on earth do you mean?'

'He killed Herb Tullos.'

The Sergeant looked round, to be sure that we were not overheard. Even so, he lowered his voice. 'How on earth do you make that out?'

We were interrupted by Alistair Wyman, who came round the corner of the clubhouse, bringing me another paper cup of champagne. He was smiling, although it seemed to be with an effort.

'Spoils for the victor,' he said. 'I'll have to go now. Douglas seems to have gone for a walk to cool off. Probably the best thing for him. He takes his sport far too seriously. We came in his car, so I'm getting a lift back into Edinburgh with one of the others. No hard feelings?'

'No, of course not,' I said, but I wondered how true it was.

'That's good. There aren't enough pretty girls around the club that one can afford to fall out with one of them.'

He forced a wider smile and turned away.

'Now tell me what you know.'

But I was looking at Alistair Wyman's departing back. 'That man hates me,' I said. 'I can tell. And I don't know why. It can't just be for beating his partner at Skeet.'

'Perhaps it's because you just go on and on not answering his questions,' the Sergeant suggested.

It took me a second or two to pin down his meaning. 'I'm sorry,' I said. 'What was the question again?'

His face took on the look of one who has bitten into a lemon. 'I want to know why you're so sure that Alistair Wyman committed Herbicide.'

The pun passed me by. 'Not him,' I said. 'Douglas Pender.'

There was a pause. Perhaps he was counting up to ten.

'All right,' he said at last, 'tell me why you're so sure that Pender did it.'

'A whole lot of things,' I said. 'You didn't tell me that you had another witness.'

'Is that why you've been treating me as if I had a social disease?' He took my hand. I resisted, but feebly. 'My dear girl, I've been telling you what I could. But I've been under very specific orders from Mr McHarg not to be too open with you. He's afraid – either that you'll talk yourself into danger or that you'll steal his thunder again.'

'I wouldn't do that on purpose.'

'You might do it in all innocence. And there have been too many instances of your father ending up in the witness box and being congratulated by the judge for making the police look like idiots. Apart from one rather juvenile witness, whose description would have fitted half the older members of the club and most of the visitors, what made you suspect Mr Pender?'

'The dog—'

'Alistair Wyman's dog.'

'—and he walks stiffly and he's good at Skeet and uses Express cartridges.'

'And do you by any chance credit him with a motive?'

'He wants to sell out to the Leisure Complex. There's a rumour that he and Mr Wyman were put in to vote for a sell-out. Mr Tullos was set against it. Somebody else said that Mr Tullos was ready to accept a backhander, but he could have changed his mind back again. It wouldn't have taken much to spark off a quarrel.'

'It never does,' the Sergeant said.

'But, most important of all, he told me that he and Mr Wyman had been together all Monday evening. But Mr Glencorse said that he met one of them on Monday evening. So they couldn't have been together.'

The Sergeant had put his arm round me in a friendly gesture, although his fingers had travelled rather further than was strictly friendly. I felt him jump and then heard

159

him swallow. 'When did Pender tell you about his alibi? And why? And does this have anything to do with why you're not very proud of the way you won?'

'He sat with me between the two rounds,' I said, 'and he was absolutely exuding malice and contempt. And he was going to be very hard to beat if I didn't rock his equilibrium a bit. I asked him whether he'd had a visit from the police and he said that he hadn't. So I suggested that he might be a suspect.'

'Did you tell him that we were studying firing-pin marks?' the Sergeant asked.

'Well, yes.'

He got to his feet quickly. I felt nearly chilled in the evening air with his warmth removed. 'There's such a thing as being almost right for the almost wrong reason,' he said. 'I've got to use my radio. Wait there.'

He vanished round the corner of the clubhouse at a full gallop.

He was gone for what seemed to be a long time. I soon gave up turning over and over in my mind his comment about being almost right for the almost wrong reason. My theory about the murder of Herb Tullos was a frail structure. Take away any one piece and the whole was destroyed.

There was something else on my mind which, from my strictly limited viewpoint, seemed to be of even greater importance.

I could not hide from myself that I was attracted to Sergeant Fellowes. I might not even know his Christian name, and the few words which we had exchanged on subjects other than murder could have passed between casual acquaintances, yet I knew that he would be fun to be with, and tender. And . . . but how does one know these things? Whose is the small voice which says, 'This person is for me?' One's own? I just knew that there was a magic spark.

160

The Sergeant knew it too and had let me know that he knew it; and he was approaching the point of doing something about it. He might invite me out for a meal or to the theatre or to meet his mother, but he was a man. He would not be satisfied with a pal who just happened to be of the opposite sex. Somewhere along the way he would expect the last barriers to fall.

Believe it or not, at that time I was a virgin. Only just, and it had been a near thing once or twice, but a virgin within the strict definition nonetheless. Most of my contemporaries had bestowed their cherries before they were out of their teens, sometimes before they were even into them. And it was not as though I were a prude. Sometimes, in my fantasies, I envisaged myself as a brilliant courtesan, decked in exquisite lingerie and driving men to the point of madness. In another mood, I had sometimes imagined being ravished, gently and beautifully, by a handsome man who, in retrospect, bore more than a slight resemblance to the Sergeant. But those two me's were kept locked up in a maximum-security boudoir in my brain and only allowed out when I was alone.

The fault, if it could be called a fault, may have lain with my parents. Theirs had been less a marriage than a passionate, physical affair going back for more than twenty years. But the most skilled practitioners are often the worst teachers. Mum's advice had left me with no doubts as to how the physical act was performed and its dangers avoided and yet with no understanding of what, physically and emotionally, I should expect to feel. My body and my emotions sometimes insisted that it would be marvellous but my mind said that it would be ridiculous and embarrassing.

Neither of them ever preached conventional morality to me. If they had done so, I would probably have rebelled. But when I turned to Dad as the usual fount of wisdom he said that I wouldn't go far wrong if I thought of sex as no more than a delicious way of saying, 'I'll love you for ever.' That, when I had thought about it enough, made sense. I had never felt committed enough to make that sort of declaration in that sort of way. Perhaps I never would. Perhaps I was mad to be wondering whether . . .

He was coming back, walking slowly. He sat down beside me. I waited and he put his arm round me again, but it was not quite the same as before.

'Douglas Pender didn't kill Herbert Tullos,' he said gently. 'He might have done. Perhaps he should have done. But he didn't.'

'Then why did he get so upset?'

'Because the motive was his and he knew that his partner, Alistair Wyman, had done the deed. We've been sure of that for a day or more, but we've been waiting for the last pieces of evidence to arrive before we moved. We'd rather hoped that they wouldn't learn of our interest in cartridges until then. None of the firing-pin imprints that we've been able to examine so far matched the Express cartridges which we found in the bin. But Mr Wyman bought another gun within the last few weeks.'

'Have you arrested them?'

'They're both . . . out of reach at the moment.'

'And is it my fault?'

His arm tightened. I knew that he was offering comfort in advance of some awful revelation and inside myself I cringed. 'Douglas Pender's sitting in his car at the front of the clubhouse,' he said. 'He's dead. There are no marks of violence on him.'

We were so quiet that I could hear the blood in my ears. 'I've killed him,' I whispered.

'No. You mustn't think that.'

'Yes. Either he had a heart attack or he killed himself. Either way . . .'

'Either way, it would have happened soon enough,' he said.

'You don't know that.'

He gave me a little shake. 'And you don't know that

it had anything to do with your revelations. We would probably have made an arrest today. If he had a weak heart, that might well have brought on an attack. We just don't know a damn thing at the moment. A police surgeon will be here soon and a Forensic team. Once we know a bit more, it may be time to wonder who was to blame. If anybody.'

The idea that my petty spite could have driven somebody out of the world I found shattering. That I had disliked Douglas Pender made it worse.

'You were egging me on,' I said in a small voice.

'I don't think that he killed himself over being beaten at Skeet by a girl,' he said gently. 'Nobody has an ego that big. They must have known that they would be suspected. I never egged you on to rub his nose in it. Nor to point out that firing-pin impressions are as individual as fingerprints.'

'No,' I said, 'you didn't. But you put me under pressure to beat him.' I felt the tears coming and for a little while I gave in to them. The Sergeant, luckily – or perhaps because of his profession – was not the sort of man who becomes helpless in the face of feminine tears. He comforted me as best he could, wiping my eyes and lending me a handkerchief; and when I recovered my composure a little I found that he was dropping little kisses around my face and neck, which began to seem more interesting than the demise of a comparative stranger. Sam, very much disturbed, snuffled at my other ear.

I got to my feet in a hurry. 'Thank you,' I said. 'You did that very nicely. Do you comfort all your witnesses that way?'

'Only the female ones. You're all right now?'

'Perfectly.'

'I don't want you to come round to the front,' he said. 'Not until the police surgeon's come and the body's been removed. I'd send you home, but there's no sign of your uncle yet. I may not be able to stay indefinitely. When he shows his face, I'll take you home.'

163

'When Ronnie goes out on the razzle,' I said, 'he may not come home for weeks. Is it all right if I go down and lock up the trap-houses?'

'I should think so. I'm sorry that I can't come and help, but I must wait here.'

I nodded, to say that I understood. 'Would you phone home for me?' I asked. 'Tell Mrs James . . . Oh, just tell her that I can't come yet because my uncle's failed to show up. Otherwise she'll fret.' I gave him the number for Briesland House.

I locked up the trap-houses and gathered the spent cartridges while bright lights came and went at the upper level. Daylight was failing but I could see enough to wander round picking up the unbroken clays. The activity died at last. Soon I noticed the Sergeant watching me from the head of the steps. I knocked off and climbed up to meet him.

TWELVE

It was almost midnight and as nearly dark as it was going to be. The sun had dipped below the northern horizon, but there was still a glow in the sky. Vehicle lights were vanishing down the road, but only the jeep, Herb Tullos's van and two cars were parked in front of the clubhouse.

I bedded Sam down in the jeep and went inside. The big room smelled of fresh tobacco smoke, but it held only an elderly man sitting at one of the tables with a plastic cup of coffee. He seemed to have dressed in whatever came to hand and he needed a shave.

'This is Doc Hathaway,' the Sergeant said. 'The police surgeon.'

The doctor nodded gloomily as if mention of his own identity had confirmed his worst fears. 'I was getting an early night,' he said. 'My first in a month or more. Now I'm wide awake and I know I won't sleep again. And I'm hungry.'

The mention of food made me realise that a long time had passed since the snack meal which I had dished up earlier and been too tense to eat. I looked at the Sergeant and he nodded.

There were eggs in the fridge. I used the microwave to thaw a packet of bacon and another of sausages from the freezer and then started a fry-up in the browning dish. Within a few minutes I was able to put a hot meal on the table.

'This is on the house,' I said. 'The club owes you

breakfast for spoiling your sleep.' When I filled my mouth the taste was so exquisite that my eyes watered.

The Sergeant was still helping himself to mustard. 'Can you say what killed him?' he asked the doctor.

Dr Hathaway swallowed his first mouthful. 'Haven't the faintest idea,' he said. 'Not my job. The pathologist may be able to tell you. This is good.' He filled his mouth again. 'I told you he was dead,' he pointed out, with the mouthful tucked into his cheek. 'What more do you want?'

'I could see that much for myself,' said the Sergeant.

'Ah, but could you? When the layman pronounces death, there's hope for the patient yet.'

We ate in silence until we had cleaned our plates. I got up, took money out of the till and fetched coffee from the machine.

'But you must have some idea,' the Sergeant said. He got up and went outside.

'That young man has too much faith in my profession,' the doctor said. 'He's due for a rude awakening, the first time he falls seriously ill.'

The Sergeant returned with a large brown envelope. 'The reason we were holding off,' he said, 'was that we were waiting for the clinching evidence. The old records had been microfilmed and later transferred onto the Police National Computer.'

'Then I'm surprised that you ever got them back,' the doctor said.

'No more than I am. But we had to get the records in order to find out where these were being held.' The Sergeant took some glossy photographs from his envelope and pushed one in front of me. 'One of my colleagues brought me this set when he came up about the late Mr Pender. Who does this remind you of?'

I studied the photograph. It was a conventional print of two police photographs showing the same man full face and again in profile. The man, who was not much older than myself, had dark, unfashionably cropped hair.

His regular features were vaguely familiar, but I could not place them.

'Imagine him older, with less hair and a broken nose,' said the Sergeant.

I tried again and it came to me. 'Douglas Pender?' I said.

'As he later became. These are photographs of Joukie Cairns.'

My mind was heavy with the weight of exhaustion. 'Who?' I said.

'You told me about him yourself,' the Sergeant said patiently.

'The man who shot Mr Tullos when he was a policeman?' I said, remembering.

'The same. His nose, among other things, was broken when he fell off the roof.'

The doctor was concentrating on his coffee. Either he already knew all this or else his interest did not extend beyond the purely medical facts. It was up to me to feed the Sergeant the questions which he obviously expected. 'Does the motive go all the way back? But why would Mr Pender – Cairns – want to kill Mr Tullos and not the other way round? But that's a silly question,' I added quickly. 'You said that he didn't.'

'Before you get into more of a tangle,' the Sergeant said kindly, 'I'll explain. Cairns had been involved in a series of successful robberies from jewellers' shops. The planner and leader was this man.' He laid another photograph on the table.

This time, the undamaged face was easier to recognise. Despite the abrasion of the years, the features were little changed and the air of suppressed energy came across even from the yellowing photograph. 'Alistair Wyman,' I said.

'Formerly Andrew Webster. He already had a record, but he seemed to be keeping his nose clean. We only got on to him through his arrangements for fencing the loot, but the same source tipped him off and he skipped out of the country. Almost none of the goods was recovered. We still didn't know who he'd been working with.

'Cairns tried to continue on his own, but he wasn't the mastermind that Webster had been.'

'Then where did he get the nickname?' I asked. ('Joukie' is a Scots word meaning slippery or crafty.)

'He probably got the credit for his partner's guile,' said the Sergeant. 'He lacked the cold, logical brain. When Tullos cornered him on the roof, he shot him and then, in his panic, he fell. He was given eight years but was out in five, after which we lost sight of him. He seems to have gone abroad, where Webster was waiting for him.

'When they thought that their misdeeds had been forgotten, it seems that they returned to Scotland, but to the east instead of the west. They set up as jewellers – perhaps because they had come to know something about jewellery, but just as likely because it gave them a chance to filter into the legitimate market as much of their old hauls as remained unfenced. And they began to live a life of quiet extravagance – good food, pricey trappings like cars and guns, and women with expensive tastes.

'They might have got away with it indefinitely except that they were elected to this club, where they suddenly found themselves confronted by the one-time Sergeant Tullos. During the competition a week ago, he told the story of the rooftop confrontation. He was making it clear that he recognised Cairns.'

'But . . .' I said. The Sergeant waited patiently while I sorted out my thoughts. 'But why did it matter so much?' I asked. 'Cairns had served his time, and if Mr Tullos knew Webster at all I don't suppose there was still a case against him.'

'And,' said the doctor, taking a sudden interest, 'Tullos couldn't sue Cairns for his damaged knee, because the right to raise an action for damages lapses after – what is it? – three years, I think. I know because I've had to give evidence in injury cases.'

'True, as far as it goes,' said the Sergeant. 'But there's another factor which we turned up when we looked back into Tullos's history. On legal advice which must have looked incompetent at the time, Tullos used his compensation under the Criminal Injuries Compensation Act to sue Cairns for damages and he was awarded a substantial sum. He was unable to collect, of course, because Cairns was a prisoner without any traceable assets, who vanished into limbo as soon as he was released.'

'The court order wouldn't be time-barred?' the doctor asked.

'No. And it would have been attracting interest at fifteen per cent for all those years. Fifteen per cent, compound! It doesn't take long to double a debt at that rate of interest. Tullos only had to take Cairns to court and he could collect a huge sum out of the apparently legitimate business. They'd be wiped out.'

'Whoo!' said the doctor. 'The legal eagle was probably only promoting himself a nice, profitable lawsuit with Tullos's compensation money, but it turned out to be sound advice in the long run.'

'Except that it got Tullos killed in the end,' said the Sergeant.

It all seemed very neat and logical, but there was something missing. It took my tired mind a few seconds to pin it down. 'That's a better motive than a quarrel over the takeover of the club,' I said, 'but it applies to both of them. More perhaps to Mr Pender than to Mr Wyman.'

'Tullos could have put their joint business into bankruptcy,' said the Sergeant.

'All right,' I said. 'So they had the same motive. Either could have gone back on the Monday, on the pretext of a round of Skeet but really to try for some reasonable settlement. After his Skeet, they spoke. A row blew up or Mr Tullos proved adamant and he was knocked on the head.'

'With the spade which he'd been using to tidy up the bed

of heather beside the Skeet ranges,' said the Sergeant. 'That much is clear. The spade had been put back in the soil, but the lab still managed to find traces of blood and skin. And a few grains of soil were impacted into the wound.'

'Right,' I said. 'Let me tell it. I don't want to look stupid all the time.'

'You don't,' the Sergeant said. The doctor, sensing something from the tone of voice, looked at him sharply.

I took a deep breath. 'The killer, whichever he was, recovered his wits and decided to make it into an accident. He chucked his own Express cartridges into the big bin. He may not have realised how individual the firing-pin imprints can be, but most of the members use the club's cartridges. According to Harry Noble, Mr Tullos was going to practise Ball-trap when the digging got too much for his back or his bad leg. He probably still had his spent cartridges in the pocket of his Skeet vest.

'The killer went down to the lower level to look for the most appropriate trap-house, and while he was there he moved the unbroken clays to a different position and put Mr Tullos's empty cartridges into the drum. He was just about to go back for the body when he heard voices and a loud laugh. A pair of lovers arrived and settled at the top of the banking where they could overlook the whole scene.

'He could have waited until they went away —'

'No,' said the doctor. He had gone back to listening with such quiet intensity that he seemed to have become part of the room.

'Why not?' I asked.

'Post-mortem lividity,' said the Sergeant. 'Right?' he added in the direction of the doctor.

Dr Hathaway nodded. 'He'd have to move the body very soon after death. Once the blood begins to settle, there's a permanent staining. If the body was moved after that process had begun and before it had finished, the signs would show that it had been moved. There would be other signs, of course, such as the disturbance of his clothing, but the postman admitted rolling the body over.'

'All right,' I said. 'So that's why he couldn't hang around. He made the best of a bad job. He hurried back to the Skeet layouts, stayed out of sight behind the safety walls and arranged the body in front of the Skeet trap-house. Then he ran to his car and drove away, without lights, to organise his alibi – hoping to hell that the couple were too busy with each other to be paying him much attention.'

I fetched more coffee. When I had sat down again I said, 'I'll accept the story. I'll accept that either . . . Do you mind if I keep calling them Mr Pender and Mr Wyman?' I asked. 'That's how I know them. I'll accept that one of them did the deed. But why single out Mr Wyman?'

'Good question,' said the Sergeant. (If he had said it patronisingly, I would probably have poured his coffee over his head, but he was treating me as one of the grown-ups.) 'Remember that the killer shot a practice round of Skeet while he prepared to open negotiations. Don't you find that significant?'

'I think I see what you mean,' I said. 'Or I see what I think you mean. From what I remember of the chat at last Sunday's competition, Mr Tullos might not have known that they were partners. But Douglas Pender would have had no reason to be circumspect. Mr Tullos would know why he had come.'

'And would have been very reluctant to let Pender use a shotgun in his neighbourhood,' said the Sergeant. 'A different sort of accident might have been arranged.'

'But is that all?'

The Sergeant grinned and shook his head. 'It's just one of – to borrow your own words – a whole lot of things. The last entry on the paper roll in the club's till was for an amount equivalent to six boxes of Express Super Competition. Douglas Pender bought one box of twenty-five cartridges off me this morning, two more at lunchtime and another before your challenge match. In other words, he buys them in penny numbers. But Wyman said that he had enough. I'm ready to assume that Wyman bought the six boxes and used one of them for the practice round. Then there's the dog.'

'But Douglas Pender told me that the dog would follow any man with a gun,' I said.

'A point. But it was Pender who your Club Secretary – Glencorse – spoke to, late that evening. Not a perfect alibi, but then, there's no single clincher—'

'Yes, there is,' said the doctor. We had forgotten him again and the Sergeant visibly jumped. 'Remember, I've just had the doubtful pleasure of examining Mr Pender's naked corpse.' The doctor glanced at me doubtfully, but I must have been looking rapt rather than shocked. 'From what you've said, I gather that your witness referred to the murderer running back towards the steps and running to the car?'

'Correct,' said the Sergeant before I could contradict.

'I haven't seen the medical records of Mr Pender, from the time when he was Cairns, but you referred to a fall from a roof. The man whose body I examined had some curious scars on his back so I took a good look. He'd had serious spinal injuries at some time and the signs of major surgery were still evident. Why he didn't end up paralysed is a modern miracle. Some orthopaedic surgeon had done an excellent job of patching broken vertebrae and fusing damaged joints. In my opinion, the man would be able to walk, if rather stiffly. But no way could he have run – or not, at least, without a rather limping, waddling action which your witnesses would certainly have noticed.'

'Bingo!' said the Sergeant. His face was tired but his eyes were still bright and lively. 'And neither of the witnesses likened him to a pregnant duck. That ties in with what we know about their characters. Cairns was excitable, Webster was the calm, cold-blooded planner.'

'I think you're wrong,' I said bravely. 'An impetuous

172

man would hit first and then come up with a half-baked pretence of an accident. And there are other things.'

I was about to tell him the other things. Mrs Hickson, for instance, had assumed that the hurrying figure was Mr Tullos – who had a severe limp. And Alistair Wyman had said something – what was it again? – something which suggested that his Skeet gun had been in Douglas Pender's possession.

But the Sergeant was shaking his head and this time there was that in his manner which made me want to slap him. At that time, I suppose, I was sensitive to any suggestion that I was immature.

'I think you should accept that the police, with their resources, are better equipped to arrive at the right answer,' he said, and in his tone was a hint of *Daddy knows best.* 'Miss Calder, for reasons of her own,' he told the doctor, 'dropped a bombshell on Cairns; and he was beginning to panic. It must have been clear to Webster, A, that we were closing in, and B, that Cairns would not stand up to questioning. If Cairns opened his mouth, Tullos's estate could still press for enforcement of the court order. His own record would certainly come out. There were still some serious charges to be brought against Andy Webster. So the idea of Pender getting into his car and popping off with a heart attack is too convenient. It doesn't convince me.'

'It doesn't convince me either,' said the doctor. 'There were none of the usual signs of cardiac arrest. Frankly, there were no signs of anything except death. The pathologist may find something, perhaps evidence that he was stabbed with a long, needle-like object from inside the mouth or up a nostril, although I think that I'd have found a trace of blood.'

'The pathologist will find the cause,' the Sergeant said cheerfully.

'I hope you may be right,' Dr Hathaway said.

The Sergeant stared at him. This, it seemed, was close to blasphemy. 'But he must! If we can't prove murder

173

in the case of Douglas Pender, the murder of Herbert Tullos could go by the board. The evidence is too flimsy. Witnesses who saw him from too far off to make an identification. The imprint of the firing-pin of his other gun on cartridges which were found at the top of the waste-bin. He could blame it on Pender.'

'He could be right,' I said. They both ignored me.

The doctor sighed. 'This isn't going to help me to get back to sleep,' he said gloomily. 'You listen to me, young man, and you may be the better detective for it, some day. Pathologists like to foster the illusion of infallibility. And on some things the profession of forensic medicine has come a long, long way. But there are areas in the cause and time of death which can still be very uncertain. And, of course, any murderer with knowledge will take advantage of those areas. I'm told that the most popular books in a prison library are those on forensic science and medicine and on general criminology. And doctors, you may care to note, get away with murder all the time.'

'You're pulling my leg,' the Sergeant said.

'I wouldn't touch your leg – Miss Calder might oblige. Perhaps I shouldn't be saying this, but many of my colleagues are not opposed to euthanasia. Legally it may be murder, but I admit that I'm in favour of it myself. If my condition is ever beyond salvation and I'm in real pain, a nuisance to my family and a misery to myself, I hope that some colleague will have the courage to put me out of it. Would you want to linger on after all hope was gone?'

The Sergeant shook his head and managed a twisted smile. 'There's no future in that,' he said. 'But how . . . ?'

The doctor shrugged. 'Novelists used to refer to a "little-known Asiatic poison", but they were referring to poisons taken by mouth. Poisons in the stomach are comparatively easy to detect. But a doctor with a moribund patient only has to give an injection among all the other needle-marks – and who's to know what was in the syringe?'

174

The Sergeant sat, dumbstruck. It seemed to be my privilege to act as feed. 'The pathologist,' I said.

He shook his head at me. 'From the moment of death, certain chemical changes begin. Even leaving out such unusual substances as succinylcholine chloride, which quickly breaks down into other compounds normally found in human tissue, an injection of almost any potassium salt into a vein would stop the heart immediately on arrival. And the first chemical changes after death produce potassium salts.'

'But where would the layman get potassium salts?' the Sergeant asked.

'Any health-food shop.'

'Wyman didn't have time to go shopping.'

'It could have been pre-planned,' I said.

It was the Sergeant's turn to shake his head at me. 'Until you spoke up, he'd no reason to believe that he was going to have any need to kill his partner. But you showed Cairns that suspicion could fall on him, and he began to lose his nerve.'

I looked at the doctor. 'What about gunpowder?' I asked him. 'That's largely potassium nitrate. There's a flask of it in the office.'

'Which is locked,' said the Sergeant gloomily.

'You're both rushing off up a blind alley,' said the doctor. 'When I mentioned potassium salts I was talking about my colleagues, confronted with a patient who was already like a pincushion. There were no needle-marks on Mr Pender – let alone a needle-mark containing the charcoal element in gunpowder, which would have made it as conspicuous as a spare navel.'

'He'd only have to shake it up in water,' I persisted. 'The charcoal would float to the top and the sulphur would sink to the bottom. And he had a boil or something on the back of his neck,' I said. 'Could that have been used to hide a needle-mark?'

'He had rather a nasty carbuncle which had recently

175

burst,' said the doctor slowly. 'I got one of the medical technicians to remove the plaster after it had been photographed. There was a substantial crater. It would certainly be difficult to find a puncture there. And it's easy to visualise the other man saying, "Let me clean it up for you. This may sting a bit."'

'Well, then—'

'But,' said the doctor (the Sergeant groaned), 'a potassium salt would have to be injected into a vein if it was to reach the heart. There are no veins in the back of the neck. If the carbuncle had been on his throat or the back of his knee . . .'

'But it wasn't,' said the Sergeant.

'An injection of air?' I suggested.

'A vein again,' said the doctor. 'And it's a common misapprehension that a little air in a vein will stop a healthy heart. Nonsense, of course. Rather than a hypodermic syringe you'd need a bicycle pump.' He yawned vastly. 'I think I might be able to sleep now,' he said, 'after our jolly little chat.' He paused and blinked at the Sergeant. 'If you'd said insulin, now, that could go straight into the muscle. The first chemical changes after death produce sugars. If either of them had been diabetic . . .'

I sat up in the hard chair. 'Mr Wyman is diabetic,' I said. 'I found him giving himself an insulin injection soon after they arrived.'

The Sergeant sat still for a few seconds. 'But if that's what happened,' he said, 'could we prove it?'

'I have my doubts.' The doctor glanced at his watch. 'I dare say that his blood sugar would be back to near normal by now. The only killers I can think of who were ever convicted of murder by insulin were convicted on other evidence – the confession of an accomplice, for instance.'

I broke into another silence. 'One dose for a diabetic wouldn't kill a healthy man, would it?' I asked the doctor.

176

'I doubt it very much. It might produce lassitude bordering on coma. But in this instance, death seems to have been fairly quick. I couldn't put a figure on it, but a substantially heavier dose would have been required.'

I turned to the Sergeant. 'Then you still have evidence. He needs his insulin to stay alive. If he goes back to his doctor and says, "I'm sorry but I've lost my last prescription". . .'

The Sergeant grabbed me by the ears and gave me a kiss which chased such matters as murder into the back of my mind. 'That might do it,' he said. 'I've already radioed to grab his other gun and keep a watch on his house. He's to be invited to the station as soon as he shows his face. That should cut him off from his spare supply if he has one. I must get on the air again.'

'You could suggest that a competent pathologist tests for insulin around the site of that carbuncle straight away,' said the doctor. 'Now if not sooner. You may be lucky, but don't hold your breath.'

'Right,' said the Sergeant. He scrambled out to his car, slamming the door behind him.

'An impetuous young man,' said the doctor sleepily.

The Sergeant returned within a few minutes. He looked perturbed. 'They fetched the Superintendent out of bed and he isn't too pleased about it. He doesn't believe me.'

'What doesn't he believe?' I asked.

'Any of it. That Douglas Pender's dead. That he could have been murdered. That we know how. That we might be able to prove it. Wyman will be snapped up if he shows his face at home, but before the Super authorises the fetching of a pathologist out of his warm bed I've got to go and spell it all out for him. You'll have to come in to Fettes Row with me,' he told the doctor.

'It's almost on my way home,' Dr Hathaway said. 'I don't know what I can tell him that I haven't already told you, but I'll come and hold your hand. Unless you'd rather have it held by Miss Calder?' He seemed to have some sort of Cupid obsession.

The Sergeant remembered me. 'You'd better come with us,' he said. 'I can't leave you here on your own. Wyman hasn't shown up at home yet. He may have gone on somewhere gambling or drinking. Killers often feel the need to blow off steam. On the other hand, he may be keeping a low profile until he can see whether we've accepted his partner's death as being from natural causes.'

'I'll have to stay here,' I said. 'My uncle hasn't shown up yet and I promised Sir Peter that I wouldn't leave the place deserted. The kids from the timeshare will be up and about soon and they're devils. I'll lock myself into the house and go home when Ronnie shows up.'

He hesitated. 'A girl alone here at night? To hell with security! I don't like it.'

I was divided between pleasure at his concern and indignation that he was treating me as a helpless little girl again. 'Look outside,' I said to him. 'The sun's coming up again already.' And indeed the short night was over and the north-east was bright. Somewhere outside a bird was singing.

He looked at me for a long moment and I almost changed my mind rather than add to his worries. 'All right,' he said at last. 'I'll come back as soon as I can. Try to get some sleep.'

I walked out to the cars with them and watched them drive away. There was still no sign of Ronnie.

An hour or two earlier, I could have dozed off on the throwing arm of a clay pigeon trap, but for the moment I seemed to have gone past my sleep. It would catch up with me later, but by then there would be helpers around to run the place. I cashed up, swept and tidied, filled the coffee machine and switched it off. The lights were still burning. I killed them too, and the clubroom was filled with the colourless light of early morning.

The working diary was open on the bar. I took a look at it and was gratified to note that four men, including the Sergeant, had booked sessions for 'supervised practice' – cheaper than coaching but amounting to the same thing.

My feet were sending messages, trying to tell me that I had been on them for too long. I flopped into one of the chairs, put my elbows on the table and rested my chin on my hands.

I must have dozed. When something awoke me, a bright sun was entering the eastern windows and splashing half-way down the long room.

The phone behind the bar was ringing. I dragged my feet over, leaned across the bar and picked it up. Janet's voice came on the line. She sounded as tired as I was and much angrier.

'Deborah?' she said. 'Your irresponsible dimwit of an uncle has cast up here. He's stotious. Drunk as a fiddler's bitch. As far as I can make out – because he sounds as if he's talking through a basket of wet laundry – he went back to his hovel before remembering that he was supposed to be here. The fact that he should be up there with you seems to have gone out of his so-called mind. If I hadn't heard him drive up, he'd have set the alarms off and we'd have had the police out here and then what would have become of him? If he tried to blow up a breathalyser, I swear that it would dissolve. I'm pushing food and coffee down his throat, but I think he'll probably sleep until Tuesday. Are you all right?'

'Perfectly,' I said. 'But things have been happening up here. One of the members has been found dead and we think that he was murdered by the man who committed Herbicide.'

The Sergeant's little joke fell as flat with her as it had with me. 'Did what?' she asked.

'Killed Herbert Tullos,' I said. 'It's too complicated to tell you on the phone. The Sergeant's gone off to help assemble the evidence and be present at the arrest.'

'Are you alone up there?' she asked sharply.

'For the moment.'

'I don't know whether I shouldn't come and join you,' she said. 'But the whole idea was that this place shouldn't be left empty.' I thought that she was torn between curiosity and a desire to get back to bed. But, in fairness, she genuinely disliked the idea of my being at the mercy of any passing rapist. Jealous, probably.

'You could always leave Ronnie propped up in the hall,' I said. 'Drunk or sober, he'd scare off any burglar. And he'll be looking for a fight when he wakes up. But don't worry about me. By the time you could get dressed and drive up here, the Sergeant might be back. Get some sleep.'

'You too,' she said, 'and preferably alone. Don't forget that you're bringing him for a meal tonight.'

'I'll try,' I said. 'But he isn't getting any more sleep than we are. Only your lord and master will be even half awake.'

'He can look your Sergeant over for me,' Janet snapped and she hung up. She hates it when I refer to Wallace in that way.

I dropped my receiver into place and drooped over the counter. But there was a dark shadow in the doorway and I suddenly snapped awake.

Alistair Wyman was standing, watching me. He had his Browning in his hands and, of the two of them, it would have been difficult to say which had the less friendly expression.

THIRTEEN

'Hullo, Mr Wyman,' I said brightly. 'You're here early.' Given a moment for thought, I would have realised that it was already far too late for any attempt to pretend a total lack of knowledge.

'Earlier than you think,' he said. 'I was listening to what you said on the phone.'

I thought back over what I had said to Janet. He would only have heard my end of the conversation, but that would have been more than enough. 'Oh,' I said.

'Exactly.' He walked slowly towards me keeping the barrels of his gun aligned on a spot between my eyes. In the lightheadedness which followed a sudden wakening from inadequate sleep, my mind took off after irrelevancies. I felt threatened, but I also felt somehow degraded. I wondered whether the supposedly phallic imagery of the gun was to blame but, looking back, the indignity stemmed from years of safety indoctrination. To have a gun pointed at me reduced me to the status of a clay pigeon.

He seemed to pick up my thought and he smirked unpleasantly. 'You're not going to say anything about guns being open and empty?'

Fear was catching up with me, but I still had my voice. 'Not just at the moment,' I said.

'Good. So we think that Doug Pender was murdered by the man who committed Herbicide do we? And who might that be?' He paused, but for once I had the sense to hold my tongue. 'Now you listen to me, my girl. I've never done time and I'm not going to start now, so if you

181

value your life don't get in my way. Empty your pockets onto the counter.'

I had very little in the pockets of my Skeet vest except keys. He picked up the car key left-handed. 'Which does this fit?'

'The jeep.'

'That'll do. They'll be on the lookout for my car and at this time of a Sunday morning the roads are too damned empty. All I need is a change of car and somewhere to lie up until there's some traffic on the roads. And possibly a hostage. Sit down.'

The barrels gestured me to a chair. I sat. I realised that I had never really looked at him before. His heavy frame was well muscled despite the small pot bulging over his belt, and he handled the $7^1/_2$ lb gun one-handed as though it had been a pistol. His head was blunt; without the customary cap I saw that he was almost bald, his scalp wrinkled and speckled with liver spots. Even at that hour of the morning he seemed to crackle with energy. He was overdue for his morning shave and the stubble gave him a seedy look. I had thought his features bland, but there was an underlying forcefulness and when I met his eyes I knew that there was somebody behind them whom I would not like. There was ruthlessness there, or even cruelty. I tried to tell myself that I was allowing knowledge to trigger imagination, and I would have liked to believe it.

He dug into the pocket of the jacket which had replaced his Skeet vest and produced a short length of nylon rope. From the grey state of it I guessed that he had cut up a tow-rope. 'Tie your own ankles,' he said. 'Give yourself a hobble of about a foot.' When I hesitated, he gave me a poke in the stomach with his barrels. 'I'm not giving you a chance to run for help. Do as I say or I'll kill you now.'

Encouraged by another prod from his muzzles, I did as he said. He made sure that I tied a dozen knots and pulled them tight. He drew a second length of nylon from his pocket and, still one-handed, tied a loop in one end.

'Put one hand out,' he said. He dropped the loop over my wrist and pulled it tight before laying the gun down beyond my reach. There would have been no point in fighting. I was no match for him in strength. Nor was I a karate expert. And I could not run. He tied my wrists with a few inches between. He jerked the knots tight; and nylon is a difficult rope to untie.

'Now,' he said. He picked up his gun again. Alistair Wyman was not a man to take risks, even with a bound girl. 'You can make me a meal,' he said. 'God knows when I'll have time to eat again.' I looked down at my hands and feet. 'You can manage,' he said. 'Don't try to make me think that you're no use to me. That could be the most serious mistake in your life. And the last.'

I shuffled behind the counter. Hampered though I was, it was not difficult to get supplies out of the freezer; and he was not fussy about the menu. When the browning dish was frying away in the microwave oven, he spoke again.

'Now money,' he said. 'I've been milking the cash dispensers, but I'll have to bribe my way abroad. I've still got plenty tucked away in foreign parts, thank God!'

I had locked most of the club's money away in the office and, despite my growing fears, I was damned if he was getting his hands on it. But because the first shooters would be certain to arrive with nothing smaller than large bank-notes, I had kept back a substantial float. I unlocked the till and dropped the keys back on the counter. 'There's only about eighty quid,' I said. My mouth was dry and my voice came out as a croak.

I could see him doing his sums in his head. 'There's got to be more than that.'

'I cashed a cheque for a member.' My voice had gone up to a squeak. I showed him Oliver Gray's cheque.

'He was buying a gun.'

'The gun was less. He wanted a couple of hundred in cash to see him through the weekend. He was taking some friends to a gaming club where they don't much like cheques. I was glad to get the cash off the premises.'

He grunted but he seemed to accept my story. My breath came more easily. He tucked the money away in a wallet which I saw was already swollen with twenties and English fifties. 'Now a drink,' he said. 'Scotch.'

I lifted a half-full bottle of Glenlivet from among the stock under the counter, the stock which was only dispensed when shooting had finished. He poured himself a glass and drank slowly.

My short sleep had done some good and my mind, aided by a rush of adrenalin, was fizzing again. That, I thought grimly, was just as well. He might, as he said, need a hostage; but once that need was past I would be no more than an inconvenient witness – and what would one more murder be to him? I fought to stay cool and to plan ahead. My ideas were few, but they were all I had.

The microwave made its beeping noise. I pulled on the oven gloves and opened it quickly. As I took out the browning dish, it was easy for my shaking hands to let the lid slide off and fall to the floor. I let him see that I was unsure what to do next.

'Leave it,' he said.

I turned towards the counter, shuffling until the rope between my ankles lay across the inverted lid. Ordinary dishes stay cool in the microwave oven but the browning dish is designed to be heated by the microwaves. I could feel the radiated heat on my ankles as I transferred the sizzling food to a plate. I hoped that the smell of the food would cover up that of the hot nylon and scorching floor tiles.

He laid his gun on the counter and began to eat. 'I phoned my wife,' he said suddenly. 'That's how I come to be here, in case you were wondering.' Then he chuckled. 'At least, she thinks she's my wife. I've a wife in Italy and another in Tangier. I only phoned her to say that I'd be late, but thank God I did! My . . . the woman said that the police had been there. They were asking about my Skeet gun and they took away my spare insulin. She thought

184

that they were still watching the house. I knew then that the jig was up. Well – what the hell? – the local business was doomed from the moment Herbie Tullos recognised Doug. But they didn't think to keep watch on the shop.' He patted his side pocket.

The heat seemed to be out of the dish-lid. I bent to pick it up. It had stuck to the nylon but I pulled it away. The nylon rope had melted almost through in two places. 'If you want coffee,' I said, 'one of us will have to go to the machine for it.'

He shot one glance at the machine, which was near the entrance door, and snuffled with amusement. 'Come round here,' he said.

He picked up his gun and changed places with me. I hobbled carefully round the end of the counter. For all I knew, the rope at my ankles might still hold a battleship – but it might as easily snap like cotton and betray my feeble preparation for escape. From behind the counter, he leaned over suddenly and grabbed the rope between my wrists, hauling until I was pulled off my feet and half across the counter. There was a beer-tap clamped to the back of the bar and he pulled the rope over it and down until he could hook it under the spout. Then he put a sweaty hand in my face and pushed me back.

He returned to the public side of the bar and passed out of my sight but I could hear him feeding money into the coffee machine.

To my fear was added the most miserable discomfort. My feet just reached the floor but unless I relieved the strain by standing on tiptoe my forearms were cut by the edge of the counter and the rope at my wrists tore at my skin. Almost immediately, my calves began to burn.

He seemed to be slow in coming back. I twisted my neck to look back over my taut arms. He was standing with his coffee in his hand, eyeing my racked body with the satisfaction of an artist who had produced a masterpiece. I tried to pull my bottom in but the counter prevented me.

He returned to the counter and sat down on the stool beside me. But before he resumed his meal he gave me a pat which I would have resented even coming from a doctor or a parent. I knew then that I was due to be raped and I felt a rush of blood to my head – not so much of fear now as of sheer fury. My previous flippant thoughts on the subject suddenly seemed unfunny, because the very idea was anathema. Mentally, I had almost promised the Sergeant that he would be my first and I was damned and double damned if Alistair Wyman was going to end my life before it had fully begun, or prevent me from bestowing my favour wherever I thought it right.

The Sergeant would be coming back. That thought might have given me hope, but in fact it was almost the last straw. I knew that unless I did something my Sergeant would arrive only to be killed.

Wyman finished his meal, drained the paper cup of coffee and refilled it with whisky. 'They'll have found my Skeet gun at Doug's flat by now,' he added bitterly. 'That's why he jumped as if you'd goosed him when you shot your mouth off about the police and cartridges. But I only bought the gun last month, so they'll have no difficulty tracing it to me.'

He thumped his fist on the counter and nearly spilled his drink. 'No matter how good the plan,' he said, 'it's luck that counts in the end. I'd have been all right if that moron hadn't lost his rag. He came to my house, whimpering. I lent him my Skeet gun and told him to go up, get in a little practice and try to bluff it out. If he couldn't convince Tullos that he was mistaken, he was to offer a cash settlement. Tullos would have seen that a wad of notes in his hand was better than the cost and delay and uncertainty of court action. But no! Doug lost his temper and swatted him with the spade and then rushed back home to phone me up and tell him what he'd done.'

Any faint pleasure that I might have had in the knowledge that I had been right and the Sergeant wrong was swamped by the confirmation of my worst fears. Mr Wyman would not be talking so freely if he had any intention of leaving me alive.

He sighed, took another pull at his drink and then patted me again. 'I told him to go out straight away and find somebody who knew him, to establish at least a partial alibi, but I knew it was too late. It was worth hanging around for a few days to see if we couldn't ride it out, but when Doug began to go to pieces I knew that was it.' He gave a sudden bark of mirthless laughter. 'I fancy that my own effort at tidying up showed a little more finesse than his. I thought I could get to his house and recover my gun before the police got there, but they beat me to it. I'd kept reminding him to bring it back to me, but the sod was too full of his woes to bother himself. It was my bad luck – and yours – that you'd seen me taking my insulin. And now I'll have to be out of the country before the insulin I've got with me runs out.'

He looked at his watch. 'Wait here,' he said. 'Don't go away. If you make a sound I'll hear you and I'll come back.' He slipped off his stool and headed for the toilet, taking his gun with him.

This might be my one, slim chance.

I kicked out with one foot and the rope at my ankles parted at one of the burns. Now I was committed.

I reached out a foot and hooked the stool closer, slowly, careful to avoid a sound. Men could relieve themselves more quickly than women. Pray God that he was conscious of hygiene and stayed to wash his hands. The foot-rail of the stool helped me to gain the height I needed but that damned rope was firmly hooked on the spout of the beer-tap and would not come free. I struggled. Seconds passed. I must be running out of time. I jerked and it came away but the fancy cover over the tap was dislodged and clattered on the floor. I heard a sudden sound from the toilet.

No time now for finesse. I bolted for the door. As I went through it, I heard him erupting from the lavatory.

Sam was barking his head off inside the jeep, but like a fool I had locked him in and I no longer had the key. Even if I had had it, I don't think that I would have let him out. There was no sense in both of us getting shot.

I ran. And as I ran, with the loose ends of nylon rope flicking from my ankles and threatening to trip me, each pace seemed to take an age and I had time to think. I thought that I hoped he still only had No. $9^1/_2$ Skeet cartridges with him. If he had BB, I was as good as dead.

I had no destination in mind, just a blind impulse to get as far away as possible and to find people. But in the early hours of Sunday morning the entire landscape was deserted. There would be people at the Leisure Centre, early riders, people setting off for distant golf dates, perhaps even a few who were going to church. The Leisure Centre was a long way off, but it seemed my only hope.

No shot yet, but I could hear his feet on the gravel. My running was hindered by my inability to swing my arms. He sounded as though he could catch me in fifty yards.

I almost ran past the Skeet layouts before I remembered that I had never got round to locking up the trap-houses after my contest with Douglas Pender. Without conscious decision, I ran for the first steel door. It was ajar. I dived inside, pulled it to and pushed down the catch of the Yale-type lock. I heard it snap into the locked position. Remembering that he might have brought my keys, I pushed the catch up again.

He arrived on the other side of the door, tried to drag it open, fitted a key into the lock and found that it would not turn and finally wasted his energy hammering on it. 'Come out of there!' he shouted.

My first attempt to utter came out as a terrified yelp. I waited until I had control of my vocal cords. 'If you think I'm coming out, you're living in a dream world,' I told him.

We breathed heavily at each other through the steel door.

The trap-house was the first in the row, the one, aptly enough, beside which Herbert Tullos's body had lain. Space inside was limited. I was in a chamber about four feet square with the large automatic trap occupying much of the space and the remainder partly filled with stacked cartons of clay pigeons. The squat trap was raised on a small pedestal and surmounted by a turret or magazine to take 720 birds in 6 columns. One of the police cadets must have refilled the magazine at the end of the afternoon, because only one of the columns was less than full.

The opening behind the trap was beyond my reach. It was already open and even if I could have reached to pull up the flap it could only have been locked from outside. The trap itself offered only partial cover. Frantically I tried to pick up a carton of clays in the hope of building some sort of barrier. But with my hands only separating for a few inches I could not take hold. And already I was too late. I tried to reach the knots with my teeth. The rope tasted like garage sweepings.

Alistair Wyman's face appeared in the opening. He had to crouch to look through, but even if that accounted for some of his flush I was still shaken by his expression. I could not have believed that I would ever see such concentrated venom in a human face. I tucked as much of me as I could behind the trap. Mum's nice clothes were being ruined but she would probably forgive me. Even if she didn't, I would rather be alive.

'Come out,' he said, 'or I'll kill you where you are. I've only got to shoot into the magazine and the bits of clay will knock you down.'

That was probably true. But I could hear something. 'There's a car coming,' I said.

'They won't pay much heed to a shot from a gun club. Are you coming out?'

I didn't answer. The longer he waited the better my chances.

He only gave me a few seconds' grace. Then, without another word, he pushed the muzzles of his gun into the opening.

The trap had been left switched on all night. In addition to the remote control there was a release button on the side and my groping fingers found it.

My vague and frantic hope was that the firing of a clay pigeon every second or so at high velocity through the opening might buy me a delay or even hit him where it hurt. But the arm of the trap, coming round with ferocious energy, caught his barrels and smacked them against the steel side of the opening. He pulled back, but not before I saw that his barrels were pinched and badly bent. Only a maniac would try to shoot that gun. If he went back to the clubhouse for a change of weapon I might have a chance to run.

A man disarmed feels castrated, Dad told me once. The ruination of his treasured shotgun wiped all sensible thought from his mind. 'I paid six grand for this gun!' he protested.

'You want me to quote you for sleeving it?' I asked. In the stress of the moment, we were both babbling.

I heard the tyres of a vehicle slide on the gravel as somebody braked violently.

It seemed a good moment to forget about icy self-control. I screamed and I went on screaming. When I paused for breath, feet were running across the gravel and I could hear another car approaching. 'He's trying to kill me,' I yelled.

The footsteps were silenced as they ran onto grass. Wyman, in a shrill voice, cried, 'Get back!'

'Awa' tae hell, ye bogger!' said Ronnie. There was a smack which made me think of a side of beef landing on concrete. Then silence.

I unlatched the door with fumbling fingers and pushed it open. I had to walk round the safety wall before I could take in the scene. Alistair Wyman was neatly laid out beside

Station Six, his jaw at a strange angle to his face. Uncle Ronnie was seated comfortably, his back against the safety wall, drinking whisky straight from a bottle.

The second car had arrived. The Sergeant, dear Sergeant Fellowes, was running across the grass. He looked at me and at my wrists. He looked at Ronnie who belched, covering his mouth politely. And he took a good look at Alistair Wyman.

'He was trying to kill me,' I babbled. 'Mr Wyman, I mean.'

The Sergeant looked severely at Ronnie. 'Has he been driving around in that condition?' he asked.

The tension was leaving me. I wanted to laugh and cry. I began by laughing. 'He saved my life,' I said, exaggerating a little. 'Do you really want an answer?'

'Not really.' He looked at me again and saw that the tears were not far away. The knots at my wrists defeated him. 'I'll get a knife,' he said. Instead, he folded me in his arms. My tied hands got in the way so he lifted them over his head.

My wrists were burning but I would not have broken the moment for the world. I was not yet ready to say, 'I'll love you forever,' but the moment was not very far away.

'It was Douglas Pender who killed Mr Tullos,' I said. 'This one told me about it.' I bit off the rest of what I wanted to say. Men do not like being reminded that you told them so.

The Sergeant thought it over and then pronounced judgement. 'Well, he would say that, wouldn't he?'

If I could have got my hands down I would have hit him. 'But it's true,' I said. 'Look at me when I'm shouting at you!'

Detroit City Ordinance 29-85, Section
29-2-2(b) provides: "Any person who
retains any library material or any part
thereof for more than fifty (50) cal-
endar days beyond the due date shall be
guilty of a misdemeanor."